SWIMMING TO AMERICA

Also by Alice Mead

SWIMMING TO AMERICA

ALICE MEAD

Farrar, Straus and Giroux / New York

Although Bay Ridge, a neighborhood in Brooklyn, New York, is a real place, the author has changed some of the geographical and other details to suit her story.

The author gratefully acknowledges Dr. Steven L. Burg, Adlai E. Stevenson Professor of International Politics, Brandeis University, for his critical reading of the manuscript.

Copyright © 2005 by Alice Mead
All rights reserved
Distributed in Canada by Douglas & McIntyre Publishing Group
Printed in the United States of America
Designed by Jay Colvin
First edition, 2005
1 3 5 7 9 10 8 6 4 2

www.fsgkidsbooks.com

Library of Congress Cataloging-in-Publication Data
Mead, Alice.
    Swimming to America / Alice Mead.— 1st ed.
        p.   cm.
    Summary: Eighth grader Linda Berati struggles to understand who she is within
the context of her mother's secrecy about the family background, her discomfort
with her old girlfriends, her involvement with the family problems of her
Cuban-American friend Ramón, and an opportunity to attend a school for
"free spirits" like herself.
    ISBN-13: 978-0-374-38047-2
    ISBN-10: 0-374-38047-3
    [1. Immigrants—Fiction.   2. Identity—Fiction.   3. Self-perception—Fiction.
4. Mothers and daughters—Fiction.]   I. Title.

PZ7.M47887Sw 2005
[Fic]—dc22

                                                                    2004053249

For Jocelyn

SWIMMING TO AMERICA

1

LINDA AND RAMÓN CLIMBED THE FENCE and slithered down the steep, weed-covered embankment at the edge of Shore Road Park. Below it lay their secret hideout over-looking Upper New York Bay. Linda's camera bumped against her ribs. She gave a loud Tarzan yell as she reached the bottom.

"Come on, Ramón. Race you to the hideout," she said.

"Nah. You're always running," said Ramón. "Race yourself."

"Okay. I will. Linda in the blue shorts is in the lead. Other-Linda is stumbling. Did she twist her ankle? Blue shorts–Linda looks good. She has a commanding lead. It's blue shorts–Linda by a mile!"

Ramón smiled as he ambled after her. Their hideout had been assembled from a random collection of boards, crates, and a blue plastic tarp left behind by a homeless person. Inside, it was big enough to hold both of them. If they wanted to sit outside, they used an old plastic milk crate and a tree stump they had pulled from the edge of the bay last June.

"Hey. Hold it, Ramón. You know what? I think maybe someone's been here," Linda said.

"No way."

"Yes. Look. My milk crate's been knocked over. And look inside it. A flattened orange juice carton."

"Oh, yeah. That's strange. I wonder who was here. A homeless guy? I didn't know they drank orange juice. It costs two dollars."

"Did you tell anyone about this place?" Linda asked, turning her milk crate over and sitting on it.

"Only my brother, Miguel."

"Ramón! Why?"

"I don't know. He was telling me how he can't stand to be home and asked me did I have some special place I liked to hang out. So I told him."

"But you can't tell people about this. You promised you wouldn't. This is the best spot in the world. I don't want anybody to come and drink their stupid orange juice here."

Linda lifted the camera strap over her head.

"Photo time? Okay, Linds. Take my picture," Ramón said, pushing up the sleeves of his T-shirt and flexing his muscles. "It's Mr. Universe."

"Hold on a sec," Linda muttered. She focused on Ramón. To his right was the ramshackle hideout. Behind him was New York Harbor, stretching up to the tip of

Manhattan with its row of tiny skyscrapers. She clicked the shutter.

"Got it," she said.

"School starts next Wednesday, you know," Ramón said, throwing a rock as hard as he could into the water.

"Yeah. Bummer. My mother wants me to buy school clothes. But I'm not going to."

"Why not? You don't want to look nice?" Ramón asked in surprise.

"Because that's the kind of thing Donna and Crissy do. And I'm not going to be like them anymore."

"No tight jeans or big-heeled sandals?"

"Nope. I'm going just like this. T-shirt. Shorts. Maybe I'll buy some overalls and work boots. Yeah. My mom will hate that."

"I don't know about you, Linda. I don't know why you fight with your mother so much."

"It's not my fault! You've seen how she is. She criticizes everything I do and makes me babysit Barbie-brained Tina. Yuck."

"Yeah, but she's your mother. She wants what's best for you. There's so much fighting in my house, it drives me crazy. You don't want things to get that bad, do you?"

Linda stared across the water. It was true about Ramón's family. His twenty-year-old brother, Miguel, was always in trouble, quitting jobs, mouthing off, hanging out with creeps, smoking dope. Miguel was slimy. Linda's mother was just bossy. And she played favorites with her and Tina. That was the worst thing.

"How come she likes Tina more than me? That's what I don't get."

"She likes you. She loves you."

"She hates me. She grounds me like once a week. For nothing."

"Well, she probably wants you to be safe. That's all."

"What are you taking her side for? Huh? Hey. Do you think someone was really down here?"

"Yeah, I guess so. Maybe somebody slept here." Ramón sat down and leaned against the tree stump. Together they watched the small waves bounce and slap into little peaks as the incoming tide and outgoing harbor current fought each other.

"Maybe I'll move here myself," Linda said.

"Yeah. It's nice and peaceful. No cars, even."

They watched two swallows with sharply forked tails swoop and dive for insects. Linda peered at them through her camera. "Being a swallow would be great. You could live underneath the Verrazano Bridge. Build a nice nest under there. That would be a cool place to live."

Ramón didn't answer. He drew with a stick in the dirt.

"Are you worried about school?" she asked him.

He sighed. "Yeah. I did so bad last year, it's not funny. And everyone says that eighth grade is really hard and that Miss Wesley is an ogre. I'm doomed."

"Don't worry, I'll help you."

"Thanks, but— I mean, I should probably stick it out on my own, right? I can't have help my whole life. Anyway, I'm not in ESL this year. I tested out of it. Can you imagine?"

"That's great, Ramón. I'm not surprised. You talk just like an American now. Hey, the school sent my parents a letter. They want me to go to a special academy. It's part of Clemens College. But why do you think Miss Wesley is going to give you a hard time?" Linda asked.

"Because I heard she doesn't like foreign kids."

"I'm a foreign kid," Linda said. "There are lots of foreign kids at school."

"You're not foreign. You speak perfect English. You know a ton of big words. What are you talking about, being foreign?"

"I just am," Linda said softly, avoiding his gaze.

"Yeah. Sure. Where did you come from, then?" Ramón asked. "Korea? Haiti? China?"

Linda pressed her lips together for a moment. "I'm not supposed to talk about it."

"You can tell me at least. Who am I going to tell?"

"I don't know how I got here. My mother won't say." Linda looked away, across the bay. "There's plenty she won't tell me. Maybe I just fell to Earth. Seventy-sixth Street, Bay Ridge, Brooklyn. Everybody out. I came from outer space. That's why I don't fit in anywhere."

"Come on. You fit in. You have the hideout. You fit in here."

"Yeah. For now I have the hideout. And if my mother knew I was down here, she'd kill me."

2

LINDA STOOD ON THE COFFEE TABLE, the same coffee table she sometimes pretended was a dog sled, which she was steering as a musher in the Iditarod. She yawned and sighed deeply. She was helping her mother, a seamstress, make alterations to a midnight-blue dress scattered with a spray of sequins. She didn't like wearing it. It was satin, sleeveless, with overly large armholes. And the dress had a musty, closety smell. Like the smell in a secondhand clothing shop.

"Ma." Linda groaned. "I can't do this anymore. I'll fall off the table. I swear I will."

"Hold still. Hold still. Hold still."

Linda yawned again. Her life was so monotonous. So boring!

"Ma, what about that letter?"

"What letter?"

"The one my school sent. The one saying I could go to Clemens Academy. Did you call about it?"

"Turn," said her mother, tapping her leg. "No, I did not call about it. That school is across town. You should stay in your own neighborhood."

Why? Why should she stay here? None of the Bay Ridge schools was challenging. Everyone knew that. And Clemens College wasn't far. The program sounded interesting. It had classes called Freedom, Social Justice, Photography. How cool was that? But, no. It wasn't going to happen.

Linda wanted to scream. Instead, she climbed into her boredom as though it were a puffy, hot sleeping bag. It was daydream time.

All the people in the world were pins. Tiny pins, but extre-e-e-emely long ones. With their tops as far away as a galaxy's arms and their points stuck in the planet Earth. The story was about people's pinny-point feet and how they got stuck in the ground when a person was born. That was the important part—where your feet stuck. That decided so much. That made her friend Donna rich. And Ramón poor.

Here came hers right now, the Linda-pin. Crossing the universe at the speed of light. Pinvisible to the naked eye. It entered the atmosphere. Smoking hot. Nee—arrrrh—ZZZZhhh—ka-boing! Jabbed into the pincushion Earth. That was her fate. And her fate was—

"Ow! Ma!" Linda rubbed her waist where a pin had pricked her skin.

"You're wobbling all over the place. Now hold still! There. Now turn. No, wait. Hand me the pincushion. It's over on the TV."

Linda frowned. Why couldn't her mother get it for herself? She was closer. Annoyed, Linda looked down at her mother critically. There was the scar, the long, white, snaky scar that stretched like a river over the landscape of her mother's face. Below her ear, forward along the jaw-bone, then disappearing over the jaw's precipice, fading away at her throat. How had her mother gotten such a thing? From a car accident? From a mugger?

"Linda!" Her mother swatted her. "You heard me."

"Okay. Okay."

Grudgingly Linda stepped down off the low table and handed her mother the pincushion. She thinks I'm a mannequin, Linda thought. Or a piece of fabric ready to be stitched and pinched, molded and folded. Well, she wasn't. She was Linda the Magnificent, a magical, miraculous pin of light that had spread across the eons, through dark stretches of time, beaming through the universe until she emerged, born as radiant energy and stardust. Linda the Awesome. The one and only. She started to dance a little, side to side, on the table. "Hey, hey, hey! Bah, bah she-boom bah, bah-booooo—"

"Stop that!" her mother said. "We'll go buy your school clothes later."

"Cool. I want to get overalls. And great big work boots."

"No work boots."

"I think work boots are nice," Linda said. "Dad wears them. He looks nice."

"He's a construction worker, not a little girl."

"I'm not a little girl, Ma. In case you haven't noticed. I'm thirteen."

"Well, you don't act it. Now, look, you made me pin this wrong. And call me Nanë, not Ma."

"You know I can't call you that—it's un-American. So *can* we get boots?" Linda persisted.

"Later," her mother murmured. "Not now. Don't bother me."

Her parents were Albanians. From that strange little country near Italy, near Greece. All Linda knew about her past, her family's past, was that her parents had left behind the mountainous, rugged land full of what her mother called the "devil people." Whatever that meant. The devil people, the betrayers, swallowed up everything. They took your goats and cows, your house and wool yarn, your brothers and your songs, and finally they came for your thoughts, so that you were left without any words.

"Hey, wake up, Linda. Turn."

Justice. Now there was a great word. A juicy-sounding word, like a fresh peach. Justice was the most important word in the world.

"Ma, please can I get down?" Linda asked. "I'm dizzy."

"All right. All right. But go get Tina her supper. It's all made. Pita and cucumber salad. Give her a little feta with it. And do the dishes afterward. I don't want to find a mess when I come in there."

"Since when do I not clean up?" Linda asked, surprised.

"You always leave a mess."

That wasn't fair, thought Linda, stepping carefully down off the slippery table. It was just that she could never clean well enough to satisfy her mother.

She entered the narrow kitchen of their basement apartment. There was barely room for a table, so they ate two at a time. They never sat down all together. Today her mother had made a flaky-crusted pita for dinner, stuffed with spinach and red peppers. But Dad wasn't home yet.

"Tina!" she hollered.

Her little sister, age five, ran skidding into the kitchen in her socks and sat quickly at the table. Linda served her, then sat down and helped herself to two big pieces of pita. It was delicious. She ate it slowly with a big chunk of feta cheese, big because no one was looking or she would have had to put some back. Feta was expensive.

As soon as Tina finished eating, she scooted off, probably to play with her Barbies. She was obsessed with the dumb dolls.

"Tina Banana, come back here!" hollered Linda. "You're supposed to help with the dishes. Or at least scrape the plates."

She waited for a response before turning on the faucet, but Tina didn't answer. Her little sister got away with everything. Tina made her so mad that it was kind of weird. Well, she wouldn't let Tina skitter away this time when there was work to do.

"Tina!" she roared as loudly as possible. "Ba—na—na!"

"Stop that noise!" Her mother hurried in and gave Linda a quick swat on the backside. "The neighbors might complain."

"So what if they do?"

"So what?" snorted her mother. "If they did, you'd find out so what."

"How come Tina isn't going to help me?"

"She's being fitted for a dress."

"She is? Wait. I don't get this. The blue one I was just wearing?"

"No. A new one. Just for her."

Ah-ha. Miss Party Clothes Tina. A new dress and can't help with the dishes. All five-year-olds need new dresses.

Oh well. Linda tried not to hold grudges. Holding grudges was the pits. Her mother did it, and Linda had sworn to herself this summer that she would never, ever be like her mother in any way. Not in one single detail.

Linda turned on the water. She squirted a few drops of detergent into the dishpan. For a moment she concentrated on seeing how high a cone of foamy bubbles would form. Then she realized that the real reason Tina Banana was getting a new dress was that Tina was the pretty one, and she wasn't. She was the daughter with . . . "the Nose." She had a great, big, bulbous honker. Like a Muppet's.

Hey! How was her nose doing anyway? The same? Different? As a rule Linda avoided mirrors and reflective surfaces. Even the coffee table top was dangerously shiny. So she hadn't checked in a while.

She cleaned one of the teaspoons with a sponge and peered into it. Uh-oh. Her nose was worse. Definitely. From the back of the spoon, it bulged at her, and her deep brown eyes receded, looking like dark, ghoulish caverns.

Her father's nose! Horrible! Unsightly and utterly horrible, and of course completely embarrassing. And eighth grade started in less than a week! How could she go to school looking like this?

Linda raced through the dishes, scrubbing the baking pan with a plastic scrubber, then dumping out the sudsy water. Now the two sponges, yellow and blue, were neatly stacked next to the hot water faucet, the table wiped clean of crumbs. The cucumber-dill salad was wrapped and waiting in the refrigerator for her father when he got home from his sandblasting job. Linda hung the dish towel neatly over the handle of the oven and hurried to the door of their basement apartment.

"Arms up, hold still," murmured her mother. "Careful, sweetie. Don't wiggle. This dress is full of pins."

Her mother was lowering a white dress over Tina's head and must have sensed rather than seen Linda speeding toward the door.

"Linda? Did I give you permission to leave this house? Where are you going? Are the dishes finished?" her mother called.

"Yes, of course. I'm only going for a walk," Linda called in return, her voice strained with impatience. "I'll be right back." Then she hurried out before her mother could argue.

The evening sunlight formed a soft yellow halo in a gentle mist, a cushion of light around each of the shade trees that lined the street. She loved evening. Yellow light was nice. At Christmas in Bay Ridge, everyone went crazy putting Christmas lights all over their homes. She and her dad walked the streets for hours admiring the vibrant colors.

Linda started to run. Ramón lived two blocks closer to the bay and one block south. Not far. Donna lived nearly half a mile north. Linda could run to Ramón's in no time, and running felt good.

She had to run. It released some kind of tension. Something extremely weird was happening to her, driving her crazy in the same way a pebble in her shoe or a particularly nasty mosquito bite or a well-placed zit could. She felt an upwelling of irritation and the urge to scream at the top of her lungs.

She should have been a pirate. A swashbuckler. She leaped to a stone wall that ran along the edge of the sidewalk, swashbuckling as she went. Swashbuckling was splendid.

"Take this! And that!" She sliced the air with her invisible sword. "Die, stupid sidewalk."

Tina was American. And that meant she was lucky forever and would have a good life. Why? Because her birth pin had landed in the United States. Not in some unknown country full of devil people. Why can't I be American, too, Linda wondered. How can that be justice for all?

But here was Ramón's building. She pushed open the front door and ran up the stairs. Apartment 4-B. Nieves. She rang the buzzer.

3

FOR A MOMENT, no one answered. But Linda could hear a radio playing, so she waited and rang again. Abruptly, the door jerked open.

Ramón's brother, Miguel, looked at her through narrowed eyes. "Yeah?"

"Hi. Is Ramón— Um, can I come in?"

He opened the door wider. "Hey, Ramón. It's your girlfriend. Linda's here."

"He's not my boyfriend, Miguel. I told you that before," Linda said.

"Yeah, yeah. Can't take a joke, huh?"

Miguel's long curly hair was wet. He crossed the room to the kitchenette and leaned against the sink, where the bottle of shampoo still stood, combing his hair back and then flicking the curls dry with his fingers. He wore a kind of hairstyle Linda hated. A mullet! Short on the sides and long in the back. There was a mullet Web site on the Internet, with photos of terrible hairstyles. She and Ramón had found it on the computer at the library one day. They'd laughed so hard that the librarian had thrown them out.

Ramón came into the living room, dressed only in faded pajama bottoms that were way too short for him.

"Hi, Linda."

"You're going to bed already?" Linda asked.

"Yeah. We get up before midnight. We have to go clean the cinema then, remember?"

"How could I forget? But I mean, even so, it's only six," Linda said.

Ramón smiled and wrinkled his nose. Six nights a week, he, his mother, grandmother, and sister, Nadia, headed over to a multiplex cinema and cleaned the theaters, returning home around four in the morning, depending on the mess. So Ramón was tired most of the time. It didn't really help him to go to bed at six or seven. Ramón said there was no way he could ever fall asleep that early, especially on a Friday night when the street outside was particularly noisy.

"Yeah. Well." He shrugged. He pulled out the sofa and

went to the closet for the two pillows and sheets—one pillow for him, one for Miguel, who refused to help them clean the cinema, even though it had been his job in the first place. He sat down on the edge of the sofa bed.

Linda noticed that his pajamas were tissue-paper thin and worn, covered with faded ships with smokestacks and red and blue flags. She said, "I was wondering if you wanted to go back down to Shore Road Park for a little while, but I guess not, huh?"

"Nah. We were just down there. Besides, last night I fell asleep in one of the theaters and my mom couldn't find me for a while. She kind of freaked out. So I gotta make sure I get some rest tonight. Gotta be sure I vacuum up my share of squished popcorn."

"Oh yeah? Who wipes up the spilled soda?" Linda asked.

"My grandma."

Miguel, meanwhile, was hurrying about the apartment, drinking a beer, shoving some loose change into his pocket. Then he sat down on the sofa bed beside Ramón and pulled on a pair of black cowboy-style boots, tugging his tight jeans over the boot tops.

"Pretty cool boots, eh, Ramón? Ya like 'em?"

Ramón smiled. Impossible as it was, he always tried not to make Miguel angry. "They look kind of expensive," he said.

"I want boots for school," Linda said. "Only clunkier. More like work boots."

Miguel snorted. "Those ought to look nice on a girl."

But he was smiling. So Linda smiled back.

"Hey. It's too hot in here. Turn up the fan, Miguel," Ramón said. "Okay?"

Miguel walked over to the rattling little fan in the kitchen window. "It's on medium, believe it or not. You sure you want it on high? You won't be able to hear yourself think."

"Yeah. Put it on high."

"I can't believe you guys are still going in to clean that cinema. What a bunch of screwballs you are."

"We need the money, Miguel," Ramón said.

"How can you get money in this country earning five or six dollars an hour? I'm gonna get this family some money, not you."

"Okay," said Ramón. "Then do it."

"Don't nag, Ramón. I don't like it. Mama nags me all day long. I don't want to hear a word out of you. You should look up to your big brother. Shouldn't he, Linda?"

"I don't know why. You don't even have a job," she said.

"Yeah, and I don't need one. They're a waste of time. So listen, you two. I'm going to be using that hideout of yours for a few days. So don't go down there, all right?"

Linda glanced at Ramón. "What? What are you talking about? You can't do that. It's ours."

"I can do it, and I am going to do it. I need a place to hang out for a while, and I don't want you guys bothering me."

Linda thought for a minute. What on earth would

Miguel do down there? "I don't get it," she said stubbornly. "I mean—why?"

Miguel looked at Ramón. "You better find a smarter girlfriend next time. This one is dumb."

"Miguel, shut up," Ramón said.

"All right. I'll tell you. I got a friend who needs a place to stay for a while."

"Well, why doesn't he stay here?" Linda asked. "With you?"

"What did I tell you?" Miguel said to Ramón. "Dumb as an ox."

"Leave," Ramón said.

"Good idea," his brother replied. He downed the rest of his beer and banged the bottle on the countertop next to the refrigerator. Jesus rattled on His crucifix above the sink. A larger crucifix hung over the sofa, as well as a tourist poster of a Caribbean beach and a black velvet painting of the Eiffel Tower.

Beside the sofa, on the one end table, stood a photograph of Ramón's sister, Nadia, in an ornate gold frame. It had been taken on her fifteenth birthday, six years before, the birthday when all the girls in Cuba wear beautiful gowns and have their pictures taken all day long. Like Ramón, Nadia had dark curly hair. In the photo, her hair was swept up in an elegant pompadour. She wore pearl drop earrings and a light blue dress with lots of netting around the low-cut shoulders.

But the most prominent decoration in the apartment was the carved relief sculpture of the Virgin, the patron of

Cuba. She was descending from the clouds, wearing a huge, fancy dress, and three fishermen were praying to her from their little fishing boat.

"Linda, you think I can't earn money? You're wrong. You guys want to see something?" Miguel asked.

"What?" Ramón asked uneasily.

Miguel sat down abruptly on the sofa bed again and smiled. His moods changed like quicksilver. Ramón said he was never sure what would happen next—explosive rage or explosive laughter. Miguel had always been moody. But now, in America, his moodiness had become dangerous.

"Never mind. Hey! I know. Let's go to a ball game sometime," Ramón said, probably hoping to change the subject. "See the Yankees. You want to?"

"No. I can watch 'em on television. What do I want to go to a game for?"

"To get out of the apartment. To see other people, other families. To find out how other foreigners here do this, how they live," Ramón said.

"Are you nuts?" said Miguel.

"No, he isn't," Linda said protectively. "I'd like to go. It sounds like fun."

"Forget it. Here. Look."

Miguel had taken out his pocketknife and pried off the heel of his boot. He pulled out a thick, tight roll of money.

"Where did you get that?" Linda gasped.

"Now, *this* is money. More than you guys will ever make vacuuming up popcorn at 3 a.m. You want to impress the women, you gotta have money. But I never leave this here in the apartment. You understand? Anyone ever comes here looking for money, it ain't here. I keep it with me. It's better that way. That way, there's no confusion, right?"

Ramón glanced quickly at Linda. He didn't answer.

"Right?" Miguel asked again. He replaced the roll of bills and stamped the heel back on tight.

"Right," Ramón answered softly.

Suddenly there was rapping at the door. Miguel strode across the room and opened it. Linda saw two guys in their early twenties, one Hispanic and one white, both wearing track pants and T-shirts.

"Oh, hey," Miguel said. "What's up?"

The Hispanic guy shoved him in the chest. "You and your friend, you said you'd do us a little favor. You said you'd drop off something for us. But that was only part of the deal."

"We—I mean I—did that. I gave you the money."

"Not all of it. What? You think we can't count?"

"I'll have the rest. Don't worry about it. I'll take care of it."

Ramón crossed the room and stood beside his brother. He tugged on Miguel's arm. "Come on, Miguel. Close the door, all right?"

But the white guy had his foot in the door and it wouldn't close. "The problem is," he said, "there shouldn't be a problem. You guys owe us a thousand dollars. We're looking for your friend, too. Where's he at?"

"Uh, yeah. Listen, there's been a little trouble." Miguel glanced at Linda and stepped out onto the landing, pulling the door shut behind him.

"A thousand dollars?" Linda said softly to Ramón. "Whoa. What's going on?" She thought of the roll of money in Miguel's boot. Did that belong to these two guys?

"I don't know. He's getting so messed up here."

"You mean he was okay in Cuba?"

"Pretty much. I mean, where there's a dictator, you have to be careful what you do. You don't dare mess up. Here, you're on your own. You can mess up as much as you want."

"What did he mean, 'there's been a little trouble'?" Linda asked.

"Who knows?"

"Well, I don't care. He can't use our hideout. I need it. He can't tell us what to do."

"Linda, just do what he says. Please? You have no idea what's going on here."

Over the rattle of the fan, Linda listened to ambulance sirens wailing, bringing injured people to St. Christopher's Hospital nearby. "I better go," she said.

"Yeah. See you tomorrow."

"See ya." She opened the door cautiously, and when she didn't see any sign of the young men, she hurried downstairs. She didn't care what Ramón said. She wasn't going to give her hideout to Miguel. She needed it to escape from her mom.

4

INSTEAD OF GOING HOME, back to the basement apartment that made her feel so cooped up, Linda set off for the park. She was longing to see the water, the bridge, the open sky. She ran all the way, climbed the fence, and slid down the embankment.

Oh, it was such a wonderful spot. The evening was cool and somewhat foggy. The lights atop the Verrazano Bridge towers flashed red to warn low-flying planes headed to Kennedy Airport. When it got darker, the cable lights would twinkle like strings of aqua-blue stars outlining the bridge structure.

Linda sat down, imagining that the tide was surging in now, pushing up small waves as it met the outrushing water. She liked thinking about the clashing and meeting of the two waters, from the sea and the land, meshing and flowing under and over each other, an invisible net of streams.

In a few days, school would start. School with its brain-crushing repetition. School all day and her mother at night. She'd be in a virtual prison.

Well, she could run away. Go cross-country to Alaska. Race in the Iditarod with a team of loyal-to-the-death dogs. Go to the moon.

She laid her head on her knees. The brown skin on her legs was dry. She made white crisscrosses in it with her thumbnail. A fence. Her skin was fencing her in, making her squished-up inside self separate from her outside self. Separating her from her mother, from Tina, from Ramón, from Donna.

And then he was simply there, a man with dark hair, walking along the embankment toward her, limping slightly. He was small, wiry, in tight jeans and a T-shirt, dwarfed by the size of the harbor and the huge arc of the bridge. Still, small or not, he frightened her. She jumped to her feet. Was this the friend Miguel had mentioned? He had to be.

His skin was pale, his nose sharply hooked; his oily hair clung lifelessly to his skull like strands of crushed plants. He paused and stared at her. Their eyes locked and at that moment she felt transposed, as though they'd changed places. She saw what he saw: a young girl with long, wavy brown hair, thirteen years old, standing at the edge of the vast bay, watching him.

Then Linda became herself again and glanced at the steeper part of the embankment. Could she make it up there and over the fence if she had to get away?

He called out. "Please! It's okay." He raised his arm, palm outward, as if to say stop.

When his arm fell back to his side, Linda saw a raw-looking cut running from the inside of his arm just above the elbow all the way down to his wrist.

"What are you doing here?" she asked.

"I not . . . errr . . . to understand. Sorry."

"Who are you?" she asked again.

He kept walking closer.

"How did you get here?" she asked.

He pointed behind him. To the bridge? To the bay? She couldn't be sure what he meant.

"From the water?" she asked. "You came from the water?"

"Yes, yes. But maybe you can . . ." He raised his cupped hand to his mouth and looked at her questioningly.

"Food? Wait. Are you Miguel's friend?" she asked.

"No. I don't know. But . . ."

He wanted something to drink or eat. Linda looked in her jeans pocket. She had a dollar and some change. Not much. She turned and gestured toward her hideout. "You're hungry, right?"

He smiled.

"Wait there, okay?" she said. But she couldn't be sure if he understood. She stood a moment longer, looking at him in frustration.

He shivered and rubbed his arms. He looked at her again and raised his eyebrows expectantly. He was hungry, that was all.

But she had to hurry. It was getting late and her mother would be furious if she wasn't back at the apartment soon. "Wait here. I'll be right back," she said.

He nodded and sat down on the grass in front of the hideout. Linda headed for the embankment.

"No! No police!" he suddenly yelled out. She turned.

Police? She didn't get it. Her mother always said to stay away from the police. Was he as crazy as her mother?

"No police, no police!" he called again. "Please."

"Okay," Linda said. "No police. How about a Coke?"

"Coca-Cola," he said, and grinned. "Okay."

Linda scaled the fence and ran to the nearest corner store. She bought a coffee and a warm Coke, and the kid at the counter gave her two cinnamon doughnuts the store owner would get rid of before closing time anyway. She told the boy it was for a homeless man down at Shore Road Park, which probably wasn't a lie. She had him put everything in a plastic bag.

Then she turned and ran back to the park.

As she slipped and skidded down the steep embankment, she looked around for the man. She didn't see him. Slowly she climbed down the last few feet and cautiously approached the hideout. He crawled to the entrance and squatted on his heels, grinning at her.

"America," he said again. "Very good."

"Yes," she said. She felt suspicious and somewhat afraid now. "But how did you get here?"

Instead of answering her, he popped open the soda can and took a long drink. He held out his hand for the bag of doughnuts, and she set it down on the ground near him.

"Here," he said, and patted the ground beside him. "You."

"No. I can't stay. I have to go home," she said.

He didn't seem at all like Miguel's other two friends. He seemed nice, actually. At least, nicer than Miguel.

Just then the deep, heart-thrilling hoot of an ocean-going ship horn reached them. The man nodded and smiled. He pointed at the bay and then at himself.

"By boat," he said. "I. From Greece."

"Greece?" Linda was confused. "You're Greek?"

"Bulgarian. Bulgaria to Greece. Now here. World traveler." He smiled and bit into the doughnut.

"Wow." Linda was stunned. He had jumped ship, she realized. He'd been a stowaway. But that meant he could be sent home again, didn't it? Didn't that mean he'd come here without a passport? That must be why he was afraid of the police.

And then a terrible memory somewhere deep inside her stirred like a sleeping animal, a lioness with golden ruthless eyes perhaps, and frightened her even more. What? she thought. What was it that happened to me? A river. Choking. Then the memory was gone.

"Come tomorrow, okay?" he said. "Brave girl. But no police. Nobody."

Linda frowned uneasily. He seemed so nice. But she felt as though something unpleasant and violating had entered her veins and was flowing through her body now. Something reptilian, snakelike, with a cold, patient, knowing stare.

"Do you know Miguel?" she asked again. "Miguel Nieves?"

"Coca-Cola is very good. Bring food," he said instead. "Okay? No forget."

Then with his eyes locked on hers, he slowly smiled. Linda turned and fled.

When she got to her street, she stopped running and walked, to slow her breathing so her mother wouldn't ask questions. Maybe he wasn't Miguel's friend. Maybe he was just some hungry, homeless guy who had gotten to the United States on a boat. And that cut on his arm? What about that?

A stowaway. It was possible. She had seen on television a stowaway who had hidden in the wheel well of a jet that flew from Asia to Los Angeles. But there was no way to know.

5

THE HARBOR MAN was the first thing Linda thought of when she woke up the next morning. This, she decided in the bright morning sunlight, had the makings of a major adventure. Hadn't she yearned for drama and excitement for years? Something that would connect her to other adventurous souls, her missing pin pals? And now, finally, something totally unexpected had happened. She had to tell Donna and Crissy. And Ramón. Except it was only a little after seven. Donna wouldn't be awake for ages. Neither would Ramón. How annoying to have sleepyhead friends.

Until now her best friend in the world, besides Ramón, had been Donna Mougalian. Donna's father was a carpet dealer, originally from some faraway place, Armenia or Iran, and they owned a rug store on Third Avenue called Mougalian's Magic Carpets. Donna had gorgeous thick, black hair that hung like a curtain on each side of her face, swinging as she walked, and her nose had not done anything alarming over the summer and probably never would.

Crissy MacGregor, with her auburn hair, curls, and freckles scattered like stars across her face, was Linda's other best friend. They'd been inseparable in sixth grade. Crissy and Donna read teen magazines and painted their nails different colors. For excitement, they called radio stations and then hung up, giggling. Heeheee.

Donna considered herself adventurous, but to Donna that meant piercing something obvious and a little disgusting, like a nostril or an eyebrow. That was no good. That kind of stuff wasn't real adventure. Real adventure did not come in a bottle of nail polish.

Linda got up and stretched. Opposite hers, Tina's bed was already empty, and the sound of morning cartoons reached her from the living room across the hall. It was a normal end-of-the-summer morning, but she felt uneasy. Not right. She sat on the edge of the bed, frowning, trying to figure out what felt wrong.

Afraid of the police, she thought. And then she tried not to think it. But the phrase wouldn't leave her mind. It was like a bad song that had gotten stuck in her head.

She went down the short hall and banged on the bathroom door. Her father was in the shower.

Linda leaned her head against the wall. Afraid of the police. She closed her eyes and saw shadowy figures, whispering, someone pushing her into a small dark space, yelling at her to be quiet, but yelling in desperate whispers. Her clothes were damp. It was hard to breathe, and she struggled to free herself. She opened her eyes. She didn't know exactly where the disturbing images came from, but she'd imagined them before. Now the harbor man, walking through the fog, crawling into her secret place— the hideout—had reawakened something horrible in her. A bad dream that she remembered, that interrupted her thoughts.

Stop it! she told herself. Never mind. Don't tell anyone where you came from. It's none of their business. That's what her mother said.

Tina is American, her mother had told her, but not you. She weighed seven pounds three ounces. Perfectly normal. Look how beautiful she is, little Tina. You see these baby photos? Even in the hospital you could see what a beautiful baby. You girls don't know how lucky you are. You're lucky you have water. You're lucky you have air. All words from her mother. Always the same old same old.

But where are my baby photos? Linda thought. Why did no one ever take a picture of me when I was born? Were they ashamed of me? Linda felt like crying.

She sat down cross-legged in the hall, with her hands clapped over her ears, her elbows resting on her knees. Her heart had started beating too fast. And she hated that. She had a secret fear button inside, and somehow the harbor man had pushed it. But whom could she talk to? Not her mom or dad. What was this nightmarish sensation of suffocation? How could she get rid of it?

Her heart thudded. Too fast. Too hard. Oh no. Oh no. She hated feeling like this. The only way she knew to stop the fear was to not think. Sing. Keep moving. Run. Act silly. Swashbuckle. Linda knew she'd feel better once Donna and Crissy had seen the harbor man, too. Then they could talk about him, and she could laugh away her fears. She absolutely had to call them.

Linda got up quickly, trying to ignore her clammy hands and rapidly beating heart. Her father had finished showering and came out wearing his terry cloth bathrobe, a Christmas present last year from her and Tina.

"All yours, my dear," he said with mock gallantry, gesturing to the open bathroom.

A shower would help. Get squeaky clean. Hey, she was lucky she had water, right? She ran to get her clothes. "It's all okay. Nothing's wrong, Linda," she muttered to herself as she searched through her dresser. "Everyone has moments like this. So stop it. Calm down and stop it. You got that?"

"I'm telling," Princess Tina said from the bedroom doorway. She calmly took a bite of a half-peeled banana. Her thick wavy hair stuck out wildly. Beautiful people weren't always so beautiful in the morning.

"Telling? Give me a break. What did I do?" Linda asked sarcastically. "Leave me alone, Tina."

"Nanë, Linda's talking to herself again." Tina padded off to the kitchen.

Linda groaned. She grabbed clean underwear, silky basketball shorts, and a tank top and hurried into the bathroom. She felt bad for the way she treated Tina sometimes, but she couldn't help it. She felt that she was on a collision course with the whole world. She slammed the bathroom door and locked it, then growled fiercely like a tiger.

"Nanë!" Tina shouted. "Linda's growling. She locked the door. She's going to get locked in. Nanë?"

"Forget everyone; forget tattletale Tina," Linda sang to herself in the shower. "La, la, la-a-a-a-a! . . . On top of spaghetti, all covered with cheese, I squashed Tina's meatball, I do what I please . . ."

"Linda, stop that noise!" called her mother, rapping on the door. "People are sleeping."

"Well, they shouldn't be," Linda muttered.

"And don't take too long in there, do you hear me? Don't waste water like you usually do. You're lucky to have it."

Waste water? Ha. Yeah, yeah. Lucky to have water. Two hundred and fifty million Americans all have water. So do we. Big deal. My mother is obsessed with water.

Linda washed her hair quickly and closed the faucets. She grabbed a bath towel, a scrunched-up, soggy one from the floor, where her father had thrown it. Usually her mother came in and cleaned the entire bathroom after he used it. Only Linda's father was allowed to be messy in their home. Oh well, as long as he paid the bills . . . That was exactly the kind of thing her mother said.

Ooooh, gross! Linda thought. Never, never, *never* would Linda make such remarks when she grew up. She would never be like her mother.

She stumbled into the kitchen, walking stiffly, like Frankenstein's monster, eyes half-closed, groping blindly for a cereal bowl. Her mom was frying eggs for her dad.

"Want some eggs?" he asked.

"No, thanks. I'm fine with cereal."

Her mother served the eggs, scraping them out of the little steel frying pan, then scurried out into the entryway and brought in his work boots. Already she had swept the whole apartment, shaken out all the rugs.

"*Eeeekkk!*" Linda screamed.

"Now what?" her mother asked irritably.

"Dad's boots—they're scaring me," Linda whimpered.

The boots were covered with grit and dust from his work. It was Linda's job every night to clean the dirt off them. Last night, with all the excitement, she'd forgotten. Great big boots. They'd be perfect for school. Ha.

"They should be scaring you. Who forgot to brush them off last night? Where were you, anyway?"

"At Ramón's." The memory of the two guys coming to the door flickered through her mind. How Miguel had smoothly stepped out and closed the door to the apartment so she and Ramón wouldn't hear what they said.

"You spend too much time over there. There's something wrong with those people, Linda. Do you hear me? They have their lives. We have ours. Donna is okay. Her father has a good business. Her mother dresses nice. The Mougalians are a nice family. But those Cubans. They are Communists. All of them. You can't trust a Communist. Are you listening?"

"Yeah." Linda rolled her eyes as she spooned her corn flakes.

Now her mom was fussing over her dad's lunch cooler

and packing a thermos of iced tea. There were two green Granny Smith apples left, the kind Linda liked the most. Her mother put them in the lunch box.

"Why are you working Saturday, Dad?" Linda asked.

"Overtime. No, no. Take those apples out," her father said. "Leave them for the girls. I'm an old man, right, Linda? What do I need apples for?"

Linda smiled.

"Look at her," her mother said. "All day, for me, there's nothing but frowns and arguing. The minute you say something, she's all smiles."

Already Linda wasn't listening. Her mother would go on like this all day. Complaining about her nonstop. She was plotting how to get the big green apple down to her hideout. But she had to wait until eight-thirty—one whole hour—before Donna woke up. They'd meet someplace else first, in front of the coffee place, Geppetto's. On Third Avenue. She'd invite Ramón, too. They could make hiding the harbor man their secret project. Maybe they could all adopt him and bring him food and a blanket. And a radio. That is, if he didn't turn out to be too much trouble.

6

AFTER A FLURRY OF PHONE CALLS, the girls met in front of Geppetto's Coffee House at ten-thirty. Ramón had said he'd join them later at the park. Donna had brought Crissy, who trotted over to greet Linda with a warm hug.

"Geppetto's is where everyone at the high school comes," Donna said. "We have to come back another time and check it out. It's full of old people right now."

The three girls cupped their hands around their eyes and peered through the window. They saw a handful of little round tables and perhaps thirty café chairs. The room was long and dark, with high ceilings. Already there was a line of customers.

"My sister Angie's been a couple of times. But, Donna," said Crissy, always the practical one, "I mean, come on. We're not high school kids. Give us some time. We're in eighth grade."

"Who wants to be in eighth grade?" Donna said irritably. "Look at me. I do not look like an eighth grader, do I? I could be twenty-one, right?"

Donna tossed her sleek black hair, which she wore parted in the middle. She looked like a model, but Linda wasn't about to say so.

"Twenty-one? I don't think so. Come on, you guys. Let's go to the park. There's something I have to tell you."

"All right, but I need to work on my tan there," Donna said. "My mom and I went to Jones Beach yesterday and my skin got so dark. Wait. Let's not go to the park. Tell us here, Linda. I'm sick of the park."

"How can you be sick of the park?"

"I just am. Who's there but a bunch of old joggers? There's nobody good."

"She wants to maximize her potential for meeting guys," Crissy explained.

"Yeah. So tell us here," Donna said. "And then we can go to the frozen yogurt place down the street instead. Their chocolate swirl is so fabulous. And it's absolutely fat-free. No flabby inner thighs, ladies. No unsightly jiggling."

"What is with you, Donna? Forget the frozen yogurt. Besides, I didn't bring any money." Linda scowled.

She felt betrayed. What was wrong with them lately? Before, if any of them had a problem, they all helped one another—with homework, parents, kids at school. Everything. They had been so close. They'd talked about what their bodies were doing, what they ate, every single word of every single argument they had with their parents.

"Come on," persisted Donna. "Tell us now. What's the big deal? Wait. I'll guess. Your parents are getting divorced."

"No!"

"Your mom's pregnant," Crissy said.

"No! And I'm not talking about it till we get to the park," Linda said stubbornly. "Ramón is meeting us down there."

"Ramón?" Donna asked. "You have to be kidding."

"What's wrong with Ramón?" Linda asked. "We're friends."

"Well, nothing's wrong with him exactly. If you— Never mind," Donna said, glancing at Crissy.

"What? If you what?"

Linda and Donna stood in the bright morning sun, glaring at each other. Donna turned away first. She reached into a tiny shoulder-bag, pulled out a pair of sunglasses, and put them on.

"Hey, guys. Let's not fight," Crissy said. "Did you see how Emily and Renée did their hair with those big plastic butterfly clips? Remember when we saw them at the beach last week? Their hair looked so good."

Donna stopped to look at herself in a store window. "Do you guys think I'm getting fat? I swear I'm getting so fat, and I don't know why." Donna pirouetted in front of them.

Crissy laughed. "It's because you're getting curvy. You're in puberty."

"Ugh. Don't use that word in my presence. It's so disgusting."

"Puberty!" yelled Linda with a trace of vindictiveness. "Pu—ber—"

"Linda!" Donna screamed. "Stop it! I refuse to become curvy. I'm going to stay flat as a pancake."

"Oh yeah? What are you going to do to stop it? Puberty is irreversible. There is no 'unpuberty.' Of course, you could bungee-cord telephone books to your abdomen and chest every night to keep them flat," Linda said.

"Yeah," said Donna. "Okay. I just might do that."

They started walking down Third to Seventy-sixth, out of habit, since that was Linda's street.

"Look at my sandals, you guys," Donna said. "Cool, or what? I just got them."

She wore big black sandals with thick heels that made her naturally long, slender legs look longer and thinner.

"They're nice," Crissy said. "Listen to this. You would not believe the fights this summer between Angela and my parents, especially my stepfather. They have gotten so strict. And now they won't let me do hardly anything because they can't control her. It's so unfair."

"I hate unfair stuff," Linda said. "I bet I hate unfairness more than anything else in the world."

But Donna wasn't listening. "This year is going to be so unbelievable, Linda," Donna said. "You watch. I have a whole new strategy I'm going to launch about how to be myself. I'm the New Me! Unpredictable, wild, daring. It's going to be so much fun. We are going to take over the entire eighth grade. The first thing I'm going to do is get a boyfriend."

"You are?" Linda stared at Donna. She had hated boys until recently. "I thought you always said boys were gross."

"Well, they are gross. But I'm going to get used to them. On the first day of school, we're going to sit with the boys at their lunch table."

"Oh my God. I feel sick just thinking about it. Anyway, if we sit down, they'll probably all get up and leave."

"No they won't. No. They. Won't."

"I don't know, guys," Linda said. "I'm not a new me. I'm Weird Me. I feel grouchy all the time, and I have weird thoughts, like daydreams, only they're so powerful. They really scare me."

"Those, Weird Me," Donna said in a fake British accent, "are musings. At heart you are a poet and you long for romance in your life. You feel unfulfilled. You think that no one understands you."

"Those aren't musings," said Crissy. "You suffer from hormone hell. Take a hot bath each night, massaging the tension points in your face and neck. Then put cucumber slices on your eyes to cool off and lie very still for twenty minutes."

"Cucumber slices?"

"Yeah. I tried it. They're very, very soothing."

"You've been reading too many women's magazines," Linda said scornfully.

But the scorn in her voice was to hide the truth. She did feel unfulfilled and that no one understood her, least of all her mother. And now, in some irreversible way, she felt herself separating, possibly forever, from Donna and Crissy, that she was following a hidden path downward, steep, dark, and narrow and rocky, while they bounced down daylit streets. What would happen to her without her two friends? How would she live? Her loneliness was, at that moment, piercing.

"Hey," said Linda, "did you ever think that there might be somebody secret hiding inside your medicine cabinet?" She was making up a story so she wouldn't feel so crazy and alone.

"What! Oh my God. Linda, shut up!"

"And if you opened the door, there was a secret person staring back at you from the other side. Only this other person didn't look like you. He was the opposite, the reverse of you. Like if you were very good, then this person would be just as evil. If you were white, he'd be black or maybe Asian. If you were tall and artistic, he'd be short and boring. And if you were a Democrat, he'd be a—"

"Okay! Okay! God. You really are Weird Me. No wonder your mom never lets you out of the house. Come on, Crissy. Let's run," Donna yelled.

They took off along Seventy-sixth Street and crossed First Avenue, racing each other down the last block to the park.

"See? What did I tell you? There is not one single guy here our age. Nobody. Not even Ramón. So? What were you going to tell us?" Donna asked.

"Look!" Linda pointed across the bay, the sweep of her arm taking in the bridge, the far shores, the gentle waves, the trees and paths of the park. "Isn't it splendid? You can come down here and write or think wild things. Let's go over by the fence."

With barely concealed skepticism, they followed her. "This better be good, Linda," Donna warned. "And hurry up because I have to go in a few minutes."

"Really? Where are you going?" Linda asked. "No. Don't tell me. Shopping with your mom."

"Right."

"Okay. I'll hurry."

The three girls drew close together.

"For a long time I've had a secret hideout. Ramón and I built it last June."

"Where?" they asked.

"Down the embankment. On the other side of this fence."

The girls peered over the fence, but their view was obstructed by tall weeds, baby locust trees, and sprawling nightshade with its bell-like purple flowers.

"Are you gonna run away from home?" Crissy asked. "Angie did when she was in eighth grade."

"No." Linda looked at them in frustration. "I'm not. Not right now, anyway. Listen, there's someone staying there now—"

"A homeless guy?" Crissy asked.

"Well, yeah, kind of."

"He's probably a psycho. Two thirds of all homeless people are psychos," Donna said. "And they won't take their medicine."

"Actually, I'm going to rescue him, sort of."

"What?" Donna exclaimed.

"I brought him food. He was practically starving. Listen. I need your help. He's hungry and needs food. I brought an apple today, but I didn't want my mom to find out."

Linda held up the green apple that she'd brought from home.

"He should go to a homeless shelter," Crissy said. "There's food there."

"He's afraid to. He can hardly speak English."

"I guess a homeless shelter would be kind of scary. I'd never go to one, that's for sure." Donna shivered.

"You would if you had to," Crissy said.

"No I wouldn't," Donna said.

"You'd have to so you wouldn't get hypothermia," Crissy argued. "Anyway, Linda, why do you have to help him?"

"Because! It's my fate. It's an adventure. Don't you want your life to be more adventurous? Aren't you bored out of your mind?"

41

"Not really," she said. "Not at all."

Linda's arms dropped to her sides. This whole morning, so far, was a disaster. Crissy and Donna weren't the least bit interested in the harbor man. And Ramón hadn't shown up at all.

Donna headed for the street and called back to her, "Linda, he's just another homeless guy. Forget about it."

But he wasn't! He'd come from the bay. From Greece. He was a stowaway, nearly starving, with nowhere to go, and a great big cut. She'd saved him. By being at her hideout at a certain time, a certain moment, he'd been saved by her! And maybe he was a prince. Dethroned, lost, in exile. In any case, his pin feet had landed in the wrong place—like hers.

Now Donna had to go home and go shopping for school shoes. Crissy, too. Linda stood in front of them. "No! Resist! Don't go. See? That's exactly what I mean. Don't. Don't go. Don't buy any shoes," Linda said. "Because if you do, you're just doing what everyone expects you to do."

"So you want to go to school barefoot?" Crissy asked. "Come on, Donna."

"I'll call you later, Weird Me," Donna said. "Let's do sleepovers every Friday like last year, okay?"

"Uh, yeah. Sure."

Sleepovers. Every week in Donna's poofy-pink bedroom. Linda didn't think she could do it. Last year was different; now she had changed. Why couldn't anyone see that?

School shoes. She wanted school shoes and suddenly

felt like running after Donna and Crissy. But she would buy boots, not shoes. Big, weird, clunky ones. She wanted people to look at her and see someone out of the ordinary. Linda the Magnificent Pin Poet. Or something.

7

So she stayed behind, looking out under the arch of the Verrazano Bridge. The bridge was big, bigger than school shoes or notebooks, or pencil zipper packs.

Vague emotions filled her, attached to the drifting of the clouds or the rippling of the waves. She felt connected to things that were larger than pink rubber erasers and red plastic see-through six-inch rulers and Wite-Out. She wanted to cross the bay like a giant with huge strides, to cross the Allegheny, the Monongahela, to Lake Erie. Beyond, through Wisconsin to Wyoming to the Grand Tetons and Yellowstone. She would adopt grizzly bears and wolves and protect them from ranchers.

Still Ramón didn't come.

Okay, then. The harbor man was her fate, hers alone, her doom, her secret guy in the medicine chest. She ran to the fence. In seconds, she was over, sliding down the embankment to the hideout. Before she even reached it, she knew it was empty.

"Hey!" she called out. "Yoo-hoo!"

The only sound was the slap, slap of waves. Thank God he wasn't here. Still, she approached the entrance cautiously. He could be asleep. But when she peeked inside, no one was there. She saw the Coke can, and now there was a plastic bottle of water.

She set her apple in the doorway to the hut and looked out over the bay, sweeping her hand across the level tops of the Queen Anne's lace at her knees. She broke off a stem of dried grass and chewed it.

She never heard him coming. He was suddenly there behind her.

"Hello," he said. Then, with careful enunciation, "How are you?"

He folded his arms and grinned widely at her. His teeth were stained yellow with nicotine, as were the tips of his fingers.

"Where were you just now?" she asked suspiciously. "Where did you go?"

"Oh," he said, waving his arm at the water's edge. "There. Walking. My English very good? I learn from black market videos."

"I brought you some food," she said.

"One fruit. Is not much."

"What?" Linda couldn't believe his attitude. "That's all we had."

"No. You have everything. America very rich country. Everybody dreams to come here. Every family to send one person here. I see in movies. Cars. Hotels. Food. Americans are fat people. You are fat girl."

Linda looked down at her normal-sized legs, then turned around in disgust and started to climb the embankment. "Drop dead," she said over her shoulder.

"Wait! Come back. No problem."

She turned around, still glaring at him. Although she hated herself for it, she was intrigued by him. He was a mystery washed up from the sea, from someplace remote and far away, totally unlike anyone she'd ever known, an antidote to laundry and dishes and babysitting. And somehow he was like her, connected to her. But she wasn't sure how.

"So, I mean, when you were in Greece, how did you get here exactly?"

"Many weeks wait for boat. Then I pay one sailor. Then six days hiding on boat. Maybe seven days. I am very sick from this." He made wavelike gestures. "Then one sailor finds me when we are here." He nodded vaguely at the harbor.

"How did you get this cut?" Linda asked, pointing to the long pink wound that ran the length of his inner arm.

"Is nothing." He shrugged. "I hide in anchor." He showed her by tucking his body up. "And captain tells sailor to throw me over."

"To drown?" Linda gasped. "To throw you overboard?"

"To die. Yes. But that sailor is good man. He ties me with barrel. But captain tries to stop me and to cut ropes with knife. He takes my money. I fight him and . . ." He pointed to his arm.

"The knife slipped and cut you?" she asked incredulously.

He nodded. "Now I in America and no money."

She thought this over for a moment. "In Bulgaria, did you have a job? Did you work?"

"Work?" He laughed. "Only to sell something."

"Like what?"

"Cigarettes. With truck. I take cigarettes underneath. Pass border. My brother and I go, take cigarettes from Turkey to Croatia. For European black market."

"Yeah?" she asked, waiting for more.

He didn't answer.

"And what happened?"

He looked at her and shrugged. "Is dangerous." He fell silent. Then he took her wrist. "Very good watch. Very nice." He tapped the dial with his fingernail.

"My dad gave it to me," Linda said. "For my twelfth birthday."

"Is easy to sell watch like this."

"Sell it? Are you crazy? Why would I do that?" She pulled her arm away. "Listen, I have to go." She got to her feet.

"No, no. No go," he begged. "My name is Andrei. You have this name here. One tennis guy. Andre Agassi."

Against her will, she smiled. "Bye, Andrei." She scrambled through the weeds.

There was really no big mystery about the harbor man. He had run away from home, that was all. Billions of people ran away. Millions, anyway. It was just that he'd run a whole lot farther. And he was a little older. She'd meant to ask him his age. But what difference did it make? She wasn't going to think about him anymore. He gave her the creeps.

•

At home, Linda called Ramón. "Where were you? Why didn't you meet me down at the park this morning?"

"Oh," he answered, "I had to help my mom. We just got in from grocery shopping."

"But you said you would— Oh, never mind." It was hard to be annoyed with Ramón for long. "Listen. I gotta tell you about this guy I met down at the hideout last night."

"What? You went down there? Linda! You think he's Miguel's friend?"

"I'm not sure. I mean I asked. He didn't seem to recognize Miguel's name. But listen to this! He jumped off a cargo ship tied to a barrel! How crazy is that?"

Ramón was quiet. Finally, he said, "He might be a criminal, Linda."

"No he's not! He's nice. Those two guys who came to your apartment, they're criminals. He's not like them at all."

Ramón sighed. "We have such a big problem here. Miguel has been fighting with my mother so much. She's so upset with him. That's why I decided to go with her to buy groceries today. To keep her company."

"Oh," Linda said, feeling guilty that she had pushed her excitement about the harbor man too hard. "Maybe I'll come over later. When I get a chance, I will. All right?"

"Sure. We can play rummy with my grandma."

Linda laughed. "Yeah. See ya."

8

SUNDAY AFTERNOON. Of all times to go clothes shopping. All the clothes would be pulled off the hangers, lying on the floor from the weekend shoppers. Linda doodled in the margin of her diary while she waited for her mother and Tina.

From her bed she yelled, "Ma, are you ready? It's getting late."

She wrote in her diary: "I'm going to find out how my mom got that scar. This mystery must be solved. By me!" She closed the diary and shoved it under her mattress.

She went into the living room, where her dad sat gently snoring in his recliner chair, the TV on low. There was a tennis match on. Linda had never tried tennis. It looked like fun. She took a few big swipes with an invisible racket, then a swooping backhand that knocked over the vase of plastic flowers.

"Ooops."

Linda's mother was also in the living room, struggling to pull up the zipper of her black skirt in the back. Her father opened his eyes. "What was that crash?" he murmured sleepily.

"Just me," Linda said, putting the flowers and vase back in place. "I'm a kid; I get to spill my milk."

"Ha, ha," her father said.

"You know what she wants to buy for school?" her

mother asked. "You know what she wants to get? Baggy jeans like a worker. Boots like a soldier. A soldier! You want your daughter going to school like that?"

"Don't worry so much, Tefta. All the kids dress like that now. Like it's Halloween. You know Halloween, right? It doesn't mean anything. They're kids. This is New York. No big deal."

"Ahhh!" said Linda's mother. "You talk American. Like you were born in Brooklyn. Not in Korce."

"Korce. Korce. Forget Korce," said Linda's father, holding up his hands. "So what if I talk American? What of it? Move, kid."

He swatted Linda off the arm of the chair so he could watch the match.

"Can't we go now?"

It was so typically Albanian of her mother to wait until the last minute for school clothes, not to plan anything, then to go rushing around in a complete panic. It was stupid to do things that way, but Linda knew her mother would never, ever change.

Linda wanted to buy oversize overalls and a pair of men's-size corduroy trousers and several shirts—men's thermal underwear waffle-type shirts. And a pair of heavy black boots with thick tread. And maybe, *maybe*, a few bottles of weird-colored nail polish to make it seem as though she had more clothes than she really did. If there was any money left over, she'd get a purse and some silver rings with lots of curlicues.

But Linda's mother wanted her to buy two dresses. All summer Linda had babysat a four-year-old boy named

Nathan, and she'd saved nearly one hundred and fifty dollars of her own money for school clothes. For this precise moment. There was no way that she could show up in the eighth grade at Mullaney in the kind of clothes her mother had made her wear last year. The other kids had made fun of her and called her "S.S." for "Sunday School."

"Come on!" Linda said, gritting her teeth.

Her mother was taking forever. She was back in the bathroom, recombing her hair and spraying cologne all over herself. Americans just used armpit deodorant. They didn't take cologne baths. Now her mom would reek.

"Ma," groaned Linda. "Don't do this. Please? Can we just go?"

They'd have to walk to Third Avenue, where the shops were, where everything was—crossing two long residential blocks. All the neighbors would see them.

Her mother had made it as far as the front hall mirror. She was layering on purple-pink lipstick, which caused Linda more spasms of embarrassment. Didn't her mother notice that no one else in the world looked like that? What did she think she was doing?

Her mother patted her hair in place and turned to fuss over Tina Banana. Tina wore pink stretch pants and a big white T-shirt. She had a shiny new white plastic purse. Her long, wavy, dark hair was neatly pulled back and held in place by a white headband. She looked cute. As always. Linda glanced at her nose in the mirror. A quick peek. Maybe she didn't need plastic surgery. Just a new hairstyle.

"Look, guys," said Linda, "this is taking forever. Why don't I just go with Donna tomorrow morning? School doesn't start till Wednesday. The stores are open Labor Day. Ma, please? Donna's a great shopper."

"I wish you'd call me Nanë like I taught you. Look at your sister. You see how quiet she is? Albanian girls are very nice, very quiet. You were brought up nice. And now? I don't think so. What's happening? It's Brooklyn, huh? Yeah. This is a terrible place."

"Oh my God," said Linda, bolting for the door.

She went outside, trying to create some forward momentum. Her mother finally followed, in heels, her black skirt, a great big Mickey Mouse T-shirt, and a glossy scarf fastened by a gold pin. Who in the world dressed like that?

"Let's see if we can find something in white," her mother said. "This is a good color for young girls. White."

Linda would prefer black. Dangly earrings, complicated rings, safety pins—gigantic ones. The trip was going to be a disaster. She just knew it.

Linda leaped up the steps to the sidewalk. Maybe she could walk fifty feet in front of her mother and sister and no one would know they were together. Maybe running away to join the circus was a good idea. She'd be a clown with huge shoes and one of those squirting flowers and five mini-clowns hiding under her enormous purple skirt. Her clown name would be Madame Schnozzola.

She started to walk faster, then stopped. What was she thinking? Not wanting to be seen with her mother and little sister? She was Albanian, and the family was a source of pride. An Albanian's family was one's whole world. Trust no one else, she'd been taught. She waited, then hooked arms with her mother and took Tina's hand.

"We'll make you both beautiful. I'm buying film for the first day of school. Two beautiful Albanian girls . . ."

Her mother never seemed to stop talking. Her words—sometimes in Albanian, sometimes in English—tumbled in Linda's head, pushing, shoving, shaping everything her mother's way, sweeping things aside that she didn't like. Did her mother understand what was going to happen here?

"Ma?" said Linda.

"What, dear?"

"I want to buy overalls."

"No. They're for farmers, not for school girls." Her mother glared at Linda.

What was the big deal, she wondered. Then she burst out, "Lots of kids wear clothes like that. If you didn't want me to be like other kids, then why did you come here? Why did you move to America? And where did you get that scar? Were you a criminal?"

Linda's mother stopped walking and angrily pulled her arm from the crook of Linda's. She hurried across the street, leaving both Tina and Linda behind, while the light at the corner changed to red.

"Why did you make Nanë mad?" Tina asked.

"I didn't."

"Yes, you did. You always do."

"Hey, Tina. Pretend the world is a huge ball of chewed-up gum, stuck full of pins, one of which is you and . . ."

Tina pulled her hand away. "I'm crossing. I want to go to Nanë. You're weird." She ran across on the walk light.

52

As Linda stood staring, she suddenly saw the harbor man, window-shopping in front of the pharmacy. She was shocked. What was he doing here? Why wasn't he at the hideout? She'd never imagined that he'd walk the streets, that he'd be standing only a few yards from her sister and mother.

He opened the pharmacy door and went in. Linda sighed with relief.

.

By the time they got home, her mother had lost all patience.

"Donna's a nice girl. That's why her mother likes to take her shopping. But not you. Yelling at me in the store. And staring at that young man in front of the pharmacy. I saw you. That's what girls who get in trouble do. Go on. You stay in your room, do you hear me?" her mother said, pushing Linda toward her bedroom.

"What did she do, Nanë?" Tina asked. "Nanë, what did she—"

Her mother slammed the bedroom door. Shut up, Tina. Shut up! Linda screamed inside her head.

Linda hated being confined to her room. It seemed as though her mother used this punishment more and more lately, that her mother cared only for beautiful Tina and not at all for her.

So what if I acted annoyed in the surplus store? I was tired of being nagged about buying boots. Why is that the end of the world? She yells at me all the time; I yell back once and get put in my room. Does she plan to yell at me for the rest of my life?

I'll run away, then. I wish I *had* said hello to the harbor man right in front of her and given her a really good scare. Then she might see that I feel like him, that I drifted here, too, from God knows where, that I'm obsessed with an ugly, creepy guy because he's nice to me and he belongs nowhere, like me.

Linda rolled over onto her stomach. On the floor beside her bed was the brochure for Clemens Academy and a letter from its director, encouraging her, Lindita Berati, top student at Mullaney Junior High, to apply to this exciting program, with a focus on the humanities and the arts, and best of all, "independent study."

She tossed the papers back on the floor and sat up full of sudden, defiant energy.

Independent study. Yes. Nobody is going to tell me what to do this year, and that includes my teachers. This year is going to be different. I will not fill in the blanks. I will lose my worksheets. I'll write crazy poetry about the man in the medicine chest. I'll subtract when it says divide.

And when they all yell at me, I'll laugh. It will be so completely funny.

9

On Labor Day, Ramón and Linda sat in his family's kitchen, staring out the back window down into the alley. There was a row of trash cans and a toolshed made of corrugated tin. Clotheslines crisscrossed between the buildings. A neighbor across the way had pots of tomatoes growing on his fire escape landing.

Ramón's mother came in, carrying a bag of groceries. "Hello, Ramón. Hello, Linda."

She began to unpack canned goods and bags of beans: white beans, red beans.

"Look here. Ice cream!" His mother showed the carton to Ramón. "Your favorite kind. Coffee fudge swirl. And I bought you a notebook. And pens. Pencils. But I didn't know what you have already."

"Oh, Mama, I can use my supplies from last year."

Nadia came out of the bedroom, where she'd been reading. "Hi, Linda."

"Go find your school things. Put everything on the table," Ramón's mother said to him. "Paper, pencils, ruler, everything."

"Mama, I have everything I need. I'll be fine," Ramón pleaded.

"Then put these cans away. Under there. How can you be fine? No ESL this year at all. How can you manage without that? You read so slow."

Ramón shrugged. "Maybe Nadia can help me."

"Nadia's busy with her own schoolwork."

"I said I'd help you," Linda said. "Sit next to me, okay?"

Ramón beamed. "Yeah, sure."

"What a smile!" Linda teased.

"Look at him," Mrs. Nieves said. "So cute."

"She calls me Moonbeam sometimes," Ramón said.

"Linda, you're a good girl, you know that? Please help my son. You know when we first came here, I was sure it was the start of a great future for us. But what did I know." Mrs. Nieves shrugged and turned away, folding her shopping bags and slipping them into the closet by the front door.

"Life here is hard for us," Ramón said. "We have a TV and milk to drink. We can buy things, which we couldn't do in Cuba. But it's not friendly around here."

His mother came back to the table and smoothed his hair. "And your brother? He's going to ruin us. Miguel is doing worst of all of us, quitting job after job. You better try hard this year, Ramón. I heard from some other parents about your English teacher, that Mrs. What's-her-name. She is very strict."

"Her name is Miss Wesley. I'll be okay, Mama," said Ramón softly. "I'm older now. And there's Linda."

"Mama, look what you did. Now he's worried," Nadia said, putting her arm around his shoulders. "You'll do fine, Ramón. He should stay home tonight, Mama, not go to work with us. Let him sleep for a change."

"You're right," Mrs. Nieves said. "Okay, Ramón. You sleep for all of us tonight."

Ramón's grandmother came in and pushed his school supplies out of the way. She sat down and shuffled a deck of cards.

"Uh-oh. My grandma wants us to play cards," Ramón said.

"Ramón," Linda whispered, "what are we playing?"

"Rummy. It's always rummy. And she always wins."

Linda picked up her pile of seven well-worn cards. Ramón was lucky. His mother and Nadia were kind to him.

Ramón drew a card and set down three jacks. His grandmother exclaimed loudly when she saw them.

There was a loud banging at the door. Everyone froze. Ramón put his cards down and crossed the living room to open it. The two young men who had come the other day pushed their way inside and began yelling at Ramón.

"Where's your brother?" the Hispanic one shouted. "He owes us money. We warned him once already and he still doesn't show up with it. Is he hiding from us? Is that his little game?"

"No," said Ramón in a low voice.

"Vete! Vete!" shrieked Ramón's grandmother.

She jumped up, grabbed a broom, and tried to push them back into the hall, shouting fearlessly at them in rapid Spanish. The Hispanic man yelled back at her briefly in Spanish as well. Then they completely ignored her and turned again to Ramón.

"We're short a thousand dollars. You understand that? Or are you too stupid?"

"I understand," Ramón answered. "But it's not here."

"We'll decide that."

Linda had shrunk back against the wall in the kitchen. She was terrified. Nadia came over and put her arm around her. Linda thought uneasily of that fat roll of money Miguel had shown them. It couldn't have been a thousand dollars, could it? He had said that he kept the money in his boot because someone might come looking for it. So maybe that *was* the money he owed these guys. And they'd said the word "hiding." All she could think of was the hideout. Maybe Miguel was down there right now with the harbor man. Maybe they *did* know each other. She wanted to say something to Ramón, but she had to keep quiet, not move, not stare.

Now the men were searching the apartment, drawers, closets, shelves, under the bed. They even checked the freezer and the fire escape. After a few moments, Ramón's grandmother regained her courage and followed them bravely, whacking them with the broom, gesturing for them to leave. But they continued to ignore her.

The white guy ordered, "Turn the sofa around!"

"Huh?" The Hispanic one stared at him. "What for?" His cell phone rang. "Wait. I got a call."

"Never mind the call. You heard me. Turn this thing around. Cut open the back."

In a matter of seconds, they had slashed the cushions and the back of the sofa, and the upholstery hung in tatters.

"Ohhh," Ramón's mother moaned. She had her hands clasped together. She raised her fists to her chin as if in prayer.

"There's nothing in this place," the white guy muttered. He grabbed Ramón's T-shirt and pulled him close.

"No! Leave him alone!" screamed Mrs. Nieves. "Don't hurt him."

"Where's the money, kid? Tell us!"

"I don't know," Ramón answered fearfully. "Honest."

"Please go now. You looked everywhere. I'm sure

Miguel did nothing to hurt you," Mrs. Nieves said.
"Your boy come into our territory, claiming he's selling better dope than us. Better? Yeah? How better? We
think he mixed something into our cocaine because now
the word is out not to buy from us. You call that nothing?
And then, on top of that, he doesn't pay us back all that he
owes us. You call stealing a thousand dollars nothing? Well,
maybe you're crazy, too. Him and you both. Maybe if you
understood what a thousand dollars meant, you wouldn't
be living with all this ratty yard-sale furniture."

At that, Ramón's grandmother grabbed the Hispanic
man by the arm and pushed him out. At the door, the
white one turned to Ramón. "Tomorrow, dirtbag. Without fail."

Mrs. Nieves rushed into the bedroom and slammed
the door. Nadia walked over to the sofa and dropped
down on the ripped masses of stuffing, wiping away tears.
"You better go home now, Linda. This is so serious. So
dangerous. Maybe Miguel is crazy. Maybe they're right.
Those two guys will be back, that's for sure."

Linda didn't know what to say. Somehow she felt sure
that Andrei was mixed up in this. It couldn't be a coinci-
dence that he'd turned up just when Miguel said he
needed to use the hideout. Besides, Andrei had talked
about the black market and selling cigarettes illegally, while
pretending to be helpless. "In America and no money."
Wasn't that what he'd said? She'd seen him walking right
into a pharmacy on Third Avenue. He must have gotten
money somehow.

Linda felt awful. She'd helped Andrei. She thought he

was cold and scared and needed food. She bought him a Coke instead of going to the police. She had been caught between his taking advantage of her and her mother's rule about never talking to the police, even when something was wrong. Her mother's rule made no sense.

Ramón's mother came back into the living room, wiping away tears. "What if they hurt Miguel?"

"It's okay, Mama," Ramón said. "I'll find him first."

He ran out of the apartment. Linda followed slowly down the stairs on her own. There was no way she could tell her mother about any of this. Her mother would probably lock her up for life if she knew. She was on her own and had no idea what to do. She walked home, and the streets seemed empty, the endless stream of cars hushed and quiet.

10

WEDNESDAY FINALLY ARRIVED. Donna stalked haughtily into Miss Wesley's room. She was late on the first day of school.

"Oh my gosh. Look, Crissy. She did it!" Linda whispered.

"What? Who? Oh. Donna!" Crissy answered.

Linda leaned forward in her seat and stared in shock. The front strand of Donna's dark, shiny black hair was bleached yellow-white and then sprayed lime green. Linda nearly collapsed in her chair, laughing. Ramón, who was sitting across the aisle to her left, smiled.

"I can't believe it!" Crissy whispered. "Her incredibly gorgeous black hair!"

"Well, Donna told us this year would be different!"

Donna sat at the last empty desk, which happened to be in the first row directly in front of Miss Wesley, their homeroom teacher as well as their English teacher. Miss Wesley had gray hair and wire-rims and wore a never-ending supply of corduroy jumpers over turtlenecks that often were decorated with teddy bears or balloons. But no one was fooled by the decorations. The infamous Miss Wesley was one tough cookie. She had a forceful, steely glare that shrank kids speechless into their seats. Her nickname was Buns of Steel because she pinned her gray hair up in a bun in back.

"Why did we have to get Buns of Steel for homeroom instead of someone cool like Mr. D.? This is going to be so awful," Crissy whispered. "What a way to start the day. Just look at her frowny, pruny face."

"Yeah," agreed Linda.

"She could at least color her hair," Crissy whispered.

Passing out the locker assignments was taking forever, it seemed to Linda. She watched Donna write notes in her notebook and hold them up so the boy behind her could read them. She was jealous of Donna's easy confidence, her sense of belonging, of fitting in. That was what junior high was all about, a seventh-grade teacher had told them last year. Trying to find out where in the pincushion, not-fair world you fit in. Maybe she would fit in at the experimental school; she felt sure she had no place here.

Linda opened one of her notebooks and wrote,

"Donna is happy and free. I don't see a time when I'll ever be." Satisfied that with this statement she had now begun her campaign not to do repetitive school work ever again, she began to draw a big fish at the bottom of the sea surrounded by wavy arms of seaweed. A stream of delicately shaded bubbles left the fish's pudgy lips and floated upward, seeking the surface.

Suddenly she heard her name being called. She had no idea why. Her locker assignment? It had to be.

"Lindita, am I to assume that your lack of response indicates that you don't want a locker this year?"

"Uh, yes. I mean no."

Everyone laughed. Embarrassed, Linda stumbled to her feet and hurried up for her locker number and combination.

Back at her seat she sighed. Ramón was drawing, too, a stubby man with a sword upraised, standing amid tall cornstalks. He gave her a shy smile, as if to say, Don't worry about Miss Wesley. We're in this together.

Linda couldn't stand the thought of being in eighth grade. She wanted to learn—that wasn't the problem—but she wanted to study someplace else. Like in a huge library. One the size of Grand Central Station with stars on the ceiling. She wanted to try new things such as peering through a telescope at a faraway galaxy or searching for ancient radio waves from unseen stars or playing the big, sad cello so that it sang like a wooden heart. All this seemed to float away from her, drifting like clouds to a horizon that she would never reach.

"Now," boomed Miss Wesley's voice when English began, "your first assignment is to create a family history project. This project will be displayed at Open House. It can be in any form you choose—poster, diorama, or video. But before you prepare this final version of your project, you must write a narration on any part of your family history and you should use a variety of sources."

There was no way Linda could do this assignment. Her mother wasn't about to tell her anything about where she'd come from. Linda raised her hand.

"Now, how is it possible that you have a question at this point?" Miss Wesley asked. "Yes, Linda. What is it?"

"Well, you're assuming everybody has a family history in the first place, aren't you?"

"Yes," said Miss Wesley, her voice becoming steely. "I am. I'm assuming that."

"Well, what if you don't? I mean what if your family came from basically nowhere?"

Buns of Steel bored her eyes into Linda's. "That is utter nonsense."

Linda felt angry.

Miss Wesley folded her arms and stared at Linda.

"Let me explain myself more clearly, hopefully to Miss Berati's satisfaction. Everyone, take notes on this. Now! Open your assignment notebooks and jot this down. Ramón? You, too. I said everyone. For tomorrow, you will write a brief paragraph or two that will tell me what your topic will be. It should be an interesting aspect of your family history. Something you find intriguing about your family. Got it? Then, on Monday, I expect an outline of your project. Understood, Linda?"

Linda nodded. She began to draw a portrait of her mother, her firm mouth, her eyes slightly glaring. Then down the side of her cheek to her chin, she drew the scar. That would be her topic. "My Mother's Scar." Probably Buns wouldn't like that, so she crossed it out and wrote "A Portrait of My Mother." There. Homework started. Now she could go back to working on her pencil-drawn fish.

A little after eleven, the three girls clattered down the back stairs to the cafeteria, which was in the basement.

"God. What a long morning!" Crissy said. "English, social studies, Spanish, study hall. Blech."

"It's having Buns for homeroom and first-period English that's so deadly," Linda said. "I thought we'd never get out of there."

"Feet on the floor, Donna Mougalian," Crissy said in a loud, nasal voice.

The girls laughed.

"Boy, it's hot down here," Donna complained. "It's so stuffy. Hasn't anyone ever heard of ventilation? I bet I have carbon monoxide poisoning. On the news last night, they did a thing saying school air is bad for you."

"Oh yeah? I can believe it," Linda said. "But the afternoon should go okay. We have Miss Lacey for math and Mr. D. for science. That's no big deal, right, Crissy?"

Crissy's sister, Angela, was two grades ahead of them. The girls used her as their inside source on teachers and their methods and quirks.

"Yeah. Angie said the only one to watch out for is Buns. She's like a spy. She wants to see de-e-e-ep inside you."

"Gross," said Linda uneasily. That didn't sound good. What if Buns pried a family secret out of her? Her mother would be furious.

They stepped into the cafeteria. The noise was deafening and the hot-lunch line snaked all the way out the door. Fortunately the girls had brought bag lunches from home. Linda remembered Donna's promise to sit with the eighth-grade boys. She hoped Donna would forget. She wasn't really in the mood to turn gate crasher right now.

But Donna hadn't forgotten. "Okay, guys," she said, grinning at them. "Don't let me down here. Today is the day all patterns are set. Trendsetters, unite! Come on!"

Daunted, Crissy and Linda looked at each other. Meanwhile, Donna was already zeroing in on a table.

"Donna, come on. There's no room there," Crissy said. "Forget it."

"No. We can squeeze in."

Donna went right over to the end of the table and tapped a boy named Ryan on the shoulder. "Excuse me, can we sit here?" she said.

Ryan moved over a few imperceptible inches, and Donna immediately sat down.

"Come on." She gestured impatiently to Linda and Crissy.

Somehow Donna managed to persuade the boys to move a little more, and finally Linda and Crissy sat down.

"I feel like an idiot," Linda said, pulling out her sandwich.

"Yeah. Me too."

"Look at Donna. Three boys are talking to her."

"Yeah, well, you don't have to worry. You have Ramón," Crissy said. "Although—"

"I do not *have* Ramón. Anyway, what's wrong with Ramón?" Linda said.

"Oh, I don't know." She shrugged and sipped her apple juice. "I mean, look at his clothes, for one thing."

"What is this with the clothes? You mean that baggy T-shirt that he has on today? Are you making fun of him because he's poor?"

"No. Of course not." Crissy nibbled at her sandwich and then shoved it back into the paper bag she had brought it in.

"Well, I think it's obnoxious. Are you guys saying stuff about me because I'm poor, too?"

"Linda! No! But I mean, your new clothes are a little weird. Like those great big work boots. What's up with that?".

"I don't know. I thought they'd be different. And kind of interesting. I didn't want to be like everyone else. I'm Weird Me, remember?"

But Linda felt the edges of what she knew, what she used to know from last year and before, sweeping away. The rules were changing, and somehow Donna knew it, and now it turned out that Crissy also knew. Linda had bought the baggy clothes because she thought they were funny, like a clown outfit to flap around in while your body went through its embarrassing changes or did whatever hormonal torture it had to do. But now she saw that truly trendy clothes weren't funny at all, that they were somehow selected according to rigid rules, invisible rules.

Rules about who was cool and who was not, in a world where Ramón was a joke.

She looked across the table and watched Donna flirting with the three boys, laughing and touching them on their arms. What was happening? The noise in the cafeteria was driving her crazy. Her life seemed to be whirling away from her day by day.

The three girls had created their own world last year. Crissy had brought a teddy bear on their sleepovers and they'd never once teased her about it. They'd shared everything in their own little cocoon. Linda had felt so safe. But that was then.

"Hey," said Crissy, "what happened to that homeless guy you were telling us about? Is he gone?"

"No, he's there. Want to meet him?"

"A half-starved, homeless guy? No way."

Linda gave Crissy a thin smile and then sank silently deep into herself, as if she were the fish she had been drawing that morning, now seeking the depths, not the surface.

11

INSTEAD OF GOING STRAIGHT HOME, Linda stopped at the Bay Ridge branch library and went to the reference desk. The librarian smiled at her.

"A report due already?" she asked.

"Yes. I need to find some photographs of Albania."

"Albania? Now, that's going to be tough."

"Why?"

"Well, because it was a closed dictatorship until the 1980s. No one could get in or out. It was Communist for forty years. Hmm. Let's see. Photographs."

The librarian clicked the keys on her computer while she waited for the titles to come up on the screen. "Here's one. Photographer Lewis Hine. In southeast Europe. After World War I. Do you want to look at that?"

"Sure. Yes, please," Linda said.

"Then there's a children's book on the country as a whole. Part of our Countries of the World series. That would be downstairs in the children's room. That would have maps, geography, general history, and climate for you. Will that get you started?"

At home, Linda sat right down to do her version of the homework. If she rushed, she would have time to go to the hideout and see if Andrei was still there. She had to confront him. He had probably lied about Miguel. She had to find out if he was causing so much trouble for Ramón and his family. Now, what to do with this crazy assignment?

Finally, Linda wrote:

A Portrait of My Mother

We have no family photos. Can you believe it? No family history. We came from nobody that I know of. So how can I do this project?

Here's one true thing. My mother always thinks of water. She's obsessed. She says, "When there's no water, you can't get clean." Over and over she says this. "*You girls are so lucky. You can wash. You don't know how lucky you are. You don't appreciate what you have.*" I am sick of hearing this. Okay with the water. Stop with the water. And okay with the lucky. Stop with the lucky.

My mother has this very interesting scar that runs down her face to her chin. She won't tell me how she got it. But she got it in Albania, a very poor country, where a lot of people still use donkeys to carry things like firewood and do farm work by hand without tractors. There are a lot of steep mountains there and even wild animals like wolves. I wish I knew how she got that scar. It must have hurt a lot.

The end.

There. That should cover it.

Linda regarded her paper, pleased with it. This was pretty good. This was how school should be. Truthful. Real. Not spouting back what the teacher wanted you to say. She put the paper in her notebook.

She opened the book of photographs she had taken out of the library. There were photographs of Albania and Greece and Macedonia.

The photographer's name was Lewis Hine, and he was helping the Red Cross bring big bags of food to the area. Some pictures were of children dressed in total rags, orphans. Diseased. Without legs. A young soldier missing an eye, using a crotched stick for a crutch. A little boy with an ax getting ready to butcher a goat. And more children. Endless lines of children. Stumbling along deserted train tracks from country to country through low, treeless mountains. This was Greece. This was Macedonia and Serbia. This was Albania. It was the right place, but the date was 1918. There were donkeys and stones, but mostly there were children, thousands and thousands, wandering from country to country. Brothers and sisters holding hands. Children wearing burlap sacks, tattered men's coats, barefoot even in winter, huddled miserably in snowy doorways. Staring back at her from the page. Not human anymore. They were blank inside with black, black eyes. Linda stared, transfixed.

What *was* this place her parents had left? Had those wandering children become the mountainous "devil people"? Had the children hidden in caves until they were grown and then come down from the mountains to seek revenge for their terrible lives? Had Linda's grandmother lived like this? How terrible.

She could photocopy a few of these pictures for background information. But what she really needed was family photos. Her mother had to have at least one or two packed away someplace. Everybody did.

Linda went to the screen door. Even though it was the superintendent's job, her mother was hosing the narrow walkway that led to the street. "Ma, I need to bring in a picture. Of your parents and you. For school."

"A picture! Are you crazy? Who has a picture? Who would have money for this in Albania? We were starving there. You know what starving means? No, of course not."

But now Linda did know what starving meant. The photos of the ragged children flashed through her mind.

She wanted to say something to her mother, to let her know she understood a little bit. Linda waited, but her mother said nothing more. Discouraged and hurt, not sure what to say, Linda wandered into the living room and sat on the sofa. It was a sectional, covered in olive green velvet with big red tasseled cushions placed at the corners. She pulled a cushion to her chest to hug.

Why does she always snap at me and ignore me, Linda wondered. It hurts me so much. What did I ever do?

Linda sat, feeling ashamed that she might have come from such a desperate background. Was her mother actually crazy? Checking the sink faucets all the time for drips? Yelling and criticizing? No one else's mother did that, that she knew of. Ramón's mother was nice. Donna's, too. She felt a shifting in her soul, a crevasse forming, a crevasse of mistrust.

But her grandmother must have been one of those ragged orphan children. Maybe she had started this chain of anger. Someone had done something to hurt her mother.

And now her mother would pass it on, and be mean to her, turning Linda's heart to stone, because the world was dangerous. Her mother would yell at her and criticize her and punish her to make her hard inside so she couldn't be hurt. And all Linda's filaments of gossamer—connecting her to the land and the clouds, to the bay, to Tina, Donna, and Ramón, and especially to her mother and father— slowly, one by one, these tiny threads would be torn and crushed by the stone.

What would happen to Linda then? Would she run

away? Start doing drugs like Rowena, an awful girl in her class?

Her mother was wrong to yell at her. That's what she had to remember, if she could. That was the only thought that helped Linda stay sane during these times. The screen door banged shut. Her mother stood the broom in the corner by the hall mirror and hurried off to sew. Linda got up, too, went into her room, pulled her camera out from under her bed.

With the camera strap around her neck, Linda wandered into her mother's bedroom and watched her there, intently sewing, her foot on the pedal, her eyebrows furrowed in concentration as she pushed the satiny blue cloth beneath the pounding needle. Linda held the camera to her face and peered into the viewfinder. This would make a great photo of her mother at work, hunched over her sewing machine—except you couldn't see the scar from this angle.

The devil people had done this, had made her mom so fierce. Her mother frowning, never looking up. Her mother sewing, her head bent low over the stitching needle, the little needle light shining on the cloth that she so smoothly pushed along. Linda rested her chin on top of the sewing machine. She stared, up close, directly at her mother's face. "Hey, Ma. Can you look up for a minute so I can take your picture?" she asked.

"No. I'm busy."

"Yeah, I know. But this will be perfect for my family project."

No answer. Linda stepped back. The needle whirred,

flashing up and down in a blur of motion. Click. The shutter closed; the film advanced.

"Ma, can you at least tell me about the devil people?" Click. The shutter closed.

Her mother didn't answer. She didn't care!

Fine! thought Linda in a flash of searing pain. Fine.

Because her mother wouldn't answer, because there was no other place to start, Linda would go and find the harbor man. Why not? She'd take his picture instead. And Ramón's. She'd photograph Ramón's whole family and maybe make her mother jealous. That might wake her up.

"Linda, move," her mother said without glancing up. "I need the light."

Linda whirled around, ran for the back door, and took off running down the street.

.

He wasn't there.

She lay on her back in the tall, dry grass, looking straight up at the blue late summer sky, tinged with hints of the faintest red. A white shred of cloud streamed long and tattered over her head. She could lie here on her back and think of words. Splendid, swashbuckling words. Skewer. Cosmos. Justice. Suffocation.

Near her ears, crickets chirped their rusty song, safely hidden in the stiff wicker web of grass.

Then she sensed vibrations in the ground and sat up quickly. There were Miguel and Andrei sliding down the embankment together. She jumped to her feet, her heart thudding. She shouldn't have been surprised, but she was.

"Well, well, well," Miguel called out. "Look who's

here. Linda the spy. I thought I told you to stay away from here. So, I guess you two know each other, you and Andrei?"

"Kind of," she said uneasily. She didn't want to tell Miguel anything she didn't have to.

"Well, get lost, okay? Me and Andrei have to take care of a few things this afternoon. It's private."

"No, no. She is brave girl. Stay here, no problem," Andrei said, smiling at her.

"Yes, problem. Now get out of here. And listen"— Miguel grabbed her arm as she hurried by—"don't tell Ramón or Nadia I was down here."

"Let go," she said, angrily yanking her arm free. "Anyway, what kind of business do you have? You don't have a job. So are you dealing drugs? And what about the money we—"

"Shut up!" Miguel hissed, squeezing her arm hard. She saw the two men glance at each other and suddenly she felt very scared.

"Okay. I won't tell Ramón anything. But you know what, Andrei? You can't stay here anymore. You lied to me. You *are* Miguel's friend. I asked you, and you pretended you didn't know him. I want my hideout back. So get lost, Andrei. Go away. You great big liar."

"Now, that's funny!" Miguel doubled over with laughter. And he kept laughing as she scrambled up the bank.

She hated Andrei. He'd tricked her. He'd probably been here for years, selling drugs. He must have faked the bad English, too.

She ran down the path, past the joggers and cyclists,

glad to be free of Andrei and Miguel, and away, away, with the wind in her hair, free of all annoying and terrible people. She ran past the elderly men, the mothers with strollers blocking the path, and out the entrance, where she nearly collided with Mrs. Maloney, their third-floor neighbor.

"Uh, hi!" called Linda, rushing past her.

"Hello, Linda. Out for some exercise?"

"Oh. Yeah. I've been running a little. I have to go now. Bye!"

"Does your mother know you're down here?"

"Yes. Bye!" Linda dashed across the street.

Since when was what she did Mrs. Maloney's business? Good grief. All she needed was for snoopy Mrs. Maloney to tell her mother she'd seen Linda running full tilt down at the park. She was so sick and tired of getting into trouble. And for nothing!

•

Linda walked slowly along Seventy-third Street to Ramón's apartment. She wondered what Miguel and Andrei were up to down at the hideout. Probably they were trying to figure out how to come up with the thousand dollars belonging to the other two men. Had Miguel lost the money hidden in his boot? But how? Cards? Another drug deal?

Miguel wasn't working and Andrei had said he had no money. In America and no money. So they had to be drug dealers. That was the only explanation.

This was terrible. She should have reported Andrei to the police the first night. Or told somebody. But who?

Mrs. Nieves? She was nice, but Ramón wouldn't have wanted Linda to say anything to his mom. And Linda couldn't go to the police. Her mother had told her not to. What if the police arrested Miguel? Then maybe the Nieves family would get sent back to Cuba. Be deported because of Miguel's criminal behavior. That didn't seem right.

What about her dad? No, he was hardly ever home. And if he knew she'd been hanging out down at the bay, he'd put a stop to it. She'd lose the hideout. Linda didn't think she could breathe without her hideout to escape to. But she wasn't sure she dared to go down there now, not after what had happened today with Miguel.

12

RAMÓN LAY ON THE NEWLY PATCHED-UP SOFA; it had been taped together with duct tape and a blanket had been thrown over it. Linda sat on the floor next to him, reading his math assignment to herself. She hadn't had a chance to tell him about what had happened because Nadia was sitting on the sofa as well, watching the news on TV. Linda was struggling to concentrate on the math homework.

"What are you going to do for your family project?" Ramón asked.

"I don't know. Maybe take some photos of my mother and put some captions with them. Plus get some photos from the region she came from."

"Can you take pictures of my family and do my outline for me?"

"Well, yeah." Linda frowned. He should at least try to do the outline himself. Then she could correct it.

"What's wrong?" Ramón asked.

"Nothing. This apartment doesn't show very much."

"You could take pictures of us cleaning the cinema. Yeah! You should see the backpack vacuum cleaner I get to put on. I'm like a space guy. An astronaut."

"Yeah. Okay." Then she stared off into space, an idea forming in her head. She could take a photo of Andrei and turn that in to the police somehow. Maybe she could mail it anonymously, with a note. That way, the police wouldn't come to her house and question her or her parents. That would solve everything! What a great idea.

"Yo! Linda! Are we doing math or not?" Ramón asked.

"Uh, yeah. These aren't so hard. You ready?"

"Yeah. I guess."

He pulled a crumpled math paper out of his notebook. He hadn't finished his math work in class, hadn't even come close. That's because it involved word problems, and he had trouble with the words.

"Okay," Linda said. "This is about two trains. So draw a picture of two trains at one train station together."

Ramón yawned. His mind seemed to wander as he drew the trains.

"Hey! You want me to help you or not?"

"Sorry. Okay," Ramón said. "Now I will concentrate.

Here, let me read. If one train leaving station A is traveling at a speed of seventy miles per hour and it overtakes another train traveling at thirty miles per hour . . . Overtakes? Linda, what's 'overtakes'? Takes over? Like a dictator takes over?"

"No. It means 'passes it.' Like two cars on a highway—one passes the other."

"It doesn't say 'passes it.' "

"No."

"But it should."

"Ramón! Just—"

They heard the rattle of a key in the lock and looked up as Miguel walked in. He wore jeans, sunglasses, and a tight white T-shirt. He was carrying two small hand weights and gave no sign at all of having just been at the hideout.

"Hey, Ramón, Nadia. Guess what? I got a job."

Linda's eyes widened. She was sure he was lying.

"You did? Where?" Ramón asked.

"Over on Eighth Avenue. A bar-and-nightclub-type place. I'm working the door. That's what these weights are for. I gotta get in shape."

He pulled out a second set of weights from the closet and set them on the floor.

"They paid me some money ahead of time so I could get this set of weights. Every day I'm gonna be lifting. By the end of the week you guys won't recognize me. I'll be packed with muscle."

Linda stifled a sarcastic snort. He was probably lifting weights so he could get strong enough to try and beat up those two guys. Maybe because he was scared of them, she thought bitterly to herself. She glared at him.

Miguel lifted the short bar over his head, then down to his chin. Up, down. Up, down.

"Hey! Cool. Let me try!" Ramón called out, jumping up.

Miguel set the bar gently on the floor. Ramón bent over and managed to lift the bigger set of weights up to his waist before he began to stagger. "Whoa! These are heavy."

"You better believe it. The best part of the job is I'm getting three hundred fifty dollars a week. And I get to watch all the beautiful women coming in and out. Some nights they'll have live music." Miguel snapped his fingers above his head and swayed his hips.

"So you're the bouncer, right?" Ramón asked.

"Just tell Mama that I'm the doorman at a restaurant. That's what I'm gonna say, all right? And if she asks you, you back me up. Just tell her I'm a doorman. You, too, Nadia. Better yet, don't say anything. I'll tell her."

Ramón dropped his gaze and nodded. Nadia clicked off the TV and sat in silence, looking straight ahead, not at Miguel.

"Yeah. Better not say anything," Linda echoed bitterly.

"Hey! Shut up, okay, Linda? Just mind your own business for a change." Miguel's dark eyes flashed a warning at her.

Unaware of what exactly was wrong, Ramón tried to change the subject. "In Cuba we used to have fun, didn't we, Miguel? Playing soccer in the streets, chasing tourists from Canada, hanging out at the seawall. Every night at nine o'clock, the cannons used to shoot off. Boom. Boom."

Nadia smiled at him and ruffled his dark hair. Miguel didn't answer.

"So, I guess . . . What's the name of the bar?" Ramón asked without looking up.

"You don't need to know that," Miguel answered sharply. "Are you working for the police? What difference does it make what the name is?"

Ramón sighed. "None, I guess."

"Leave him alone, Miguel," Nadia said. "You're so bad-tempered."

"Listen. You know which one of us is going to get us out of this ugly little apartment? It's gonna be me. Not you, Nadia. You should forget this training class in computers. You went for an interview the other day, right? Did anyone call you back? No. Nobody's going to hire you. You have an accent. You're foreign. Nobody wants foreign-accent voices answering their telephones. What company is willing to risk that? And listen, Linda, find something else to do besides hang around here. Don't you have any girlfriends? I don't want to find you here all the time."

Linda looked down at her boots, her lips pressed tightly together.

"Miguel, shut up!" Ramón said angrily. "It's none of your business if me and Linda are friends. We're doing homework now. What's it to you?"

They all heard Mrs. Nieves's heavy steps on the staircase, then the rattle of the door key. Miguel hurried to the dresser. He pulled out a clean T-shirt and tossed the one he had on in the laundry basket. He moved so fast that when his mother finally opened the door, he was already on his way out.

"Miguel!" she called.

He hurried down the stairs. She leaned over the railing. "Miguel! Where are you going? What about the cinema? One day the owner will show up. It's your job, not ours. So what will I tell him, huh? That you are lazy and no good? Huh? And those guys. If they come today. What did you do with their money? Ahhhh!"

She came in, followed by Ramón's grandmother.

"Why do I bother talking to him? He hears nothing. He cares about nothing. Where did he learn to behave this way? How could I have raised a child like this?"

Ramón glanced down at his train math problem, afraid that his mother would start in on him next.

"Look at this one," his mother said. "He still didn't finish his math today. Did you try hard in school, Moonbeam?"

Ramón nodded.

"Good. That's all I ask. Do your best every day, and you'll make God and your mother very happy."

Linda whispered, "Hey, Ramón, let me take your paper home. I have to go now."

"Okay. And can you do my outline for Monday?"

"Yeah. Come on downstairs with me. So, ummm . . . Bye, Mrs. Nieves."

"Bye-bye, Linda."

At the bottom of the stairs, Linda turned. She couldn't let Ramón believe all of Miguel's lies. She had to tell him. "Ramón, listen. Earlier I saw Miguel down at the hideout with the other guy, Andrei. You know, the guy who said he came from Bulgaria? The stowaway? They have some kind of business deal, and they told me to leave. I don't think he has a job at a bar at all."

"A business deal?" Ramón asked. "Like what?"

"How should I know?" Linda said glumly. "But I bet it involves a thousand dollars."

"Not a legal business deal."

"No. Probably he's trying to get money to pay the guys who ripped up your sofa. Miguel must be hiding that money we saw in his boot from those guys. Andrei and Miguel were so mad at me for being down there. It was scary. Maybe we should tell your mother," Linda suggested.

"No, Linda! Don't. No way. She'd be furious. There would be a fight here like you can't imagine. And Miguel will know it was you who told. He'll beat me up, for sure."

"He beats you up?" Linda asked.

"Yeah, sometimes. He has a pretty bad temper. Don't tell anybody right now, Linda. Let's wait a little and see. Maybe it's nothing, you know? Maybe it's just talk. That's how it is a lot of times with Miguel. He's just talking. He'll give them what he owes them. Then, when this blows over, we'll tell my mother for sure. Okay? Please let it go."

13

THURSDAY PASSED IN A SLOW-MOTION BLUR. Linda went straight home after school. Her mother needed her to watch Tina while she dropped off the sequined blue dress. And besides, Linda was hoping to intercept a call from nosy Mrs. Maloney. She put on a video for Tina.

Linda was worried sick about the chaos unfolding at Ramón's house. Maybe she should completely forget the hideout, the sunsets, the swooping swallows, the bay. Yes. She would hold herself in. Behave as others wanted her to. Become a boring and predictable robot.

Restlessly, Linda paced the apartment, tossing Barbie dolls in the air as though she were a twirler in a marching band. Tina forgot the video and ran after her, shrieking, and gathered them up protectively as they hit the floor.

At four-thirty the phone rang. Linda dashed to answer it. It was Donna inviting her to sleep over on Friday. Linda agreed to come, but the idea depressed her further. She knew exactly what would happen—what kind of video they would watch: a romantic comedy; what kind of pizza they would eat: double cheese with meatballs. She threw herself on the sofa and stared at the ceiling in despair, barely noticing as Tina pummeled her legs with Barbies.

The phone rang again. Linda pounced on it.

"Linda?"

To her horror, she realized it was Buns of Steel. What

on earth could she want? Was it regarding the homework she had turned in about her mother?

"Oh. Hi."

"I liked your topic," Miss Wesley said. "Are things going okay with your outline? Do you have enough material?"

"Yeah," said Linda.

"Good. I'm looking forward to seeing what you come up with. Actually, I'm calling because we just finished a team meeting here at school. Do you know if your parents received a letter from the director of Clemens Academy, inviting you to apply?"

"Yes. We got it."

"Well, I'm asking because the school never heard back from your family. Have you talked it over? The teachers here think you would be an ideal candidate."

Had her family talked it over? Was that a way to describe the conversations in this house? Linda took a big breath. She decided to tell Miss Wesley what she thought. "I, umm, I was kind of interested. But my mom said I couldn't go."

"Oh? Why?"

"She said it was too far."

"Oh, Linda. For heaven's sake," scoffed Miss Wesley.

"I know. But that's how she thinks."

"Can you ask her to call me tomorrow?"

"Yeah. But I'm not sure she . . . Yeah, I'll tell her."

After she hung up, Linda felt guilty that her teachers were working so hard, when all she did was blow them off. So she got out her schoolbooks and did her vocabulary homework and Ramón's as well.

Just as she finished, her mother entered the living room with a new armload of ladies' clothing to be altered.

"Hi, Ma. Can I go to a sleepover at Donna's tomorrow?" Linda asked. "I told her I could. It's okay, right? Oh, and my teacher called. She wants you to call her back."

"What for? Are you in trouble?"

"No! Jeez."

"What did she want, then?"

"To talk about that Clemens program with you."

"No. There's no need to call her. I said no."

Who could call this "talking things over"? Linda buried her face in her arms.

Friday afternoon, Linda had to watch Tina for half an hour while her mother went to the dry cleaner's. The phone rang as she was flinging clothes from her bottom drawer, looking for her nice pajamas. She dashed to the living room to answer it.

"Hello?"

"Hello, Linda. This is Mrs. Maloney. Is your mother there?"

"Uh, no. She's out for a little while."

"All right. Tell her I called. I'll call back."

Linda's heart sank. It had been a couple of days since she'd run into Mrs. Maloney at the park, and she'd stopped worrying about a call from her. What on earth was the big deal about running around Shore Road Park by herself?

She was in eighth grade, for Pete's sake, not kindergarten. Why couldn't Mrs. Maloney mind her own business? She pulled out her pajamas and slammed the drawer shut. Now her mother would be angry, and she'd be even angrier when Linda told her that she was going to take photographs of Ramón's family at their cinema job. After midnight!

When her mother returned, Linda quickly set off for Donna's house, thinking of all the things she had to do in the next few days. She had to buy a couple of new rolls of high-speed film, try to photograph Andrei, her mother, Ramón. She had to return the Lewis Hine book of photos. Read the book on Albania. Do the outline. And fend off busybody attacks from that great big schnozzola-head, Mrs. Maloney.

Linda rang Donna's doorbell. A chime like Big Ben sounded. Donna's mom opened the door, then scooped up their fluffy white cat, Snowball.

"Go on upstairs, Linda. Crissy's already here."

As she entered Donna's bedroom, Linda decided that she didn't want to sleep over with Donna and Crissy ever again. She felt hemmed in here, the way she did when she was modeling a dress for her mom, gussied up, as though she couldn't breathe. Suffocating. Donna's pale pink, polka-dotted curtains seemed to bulge at her from the neat, white trimmed windowpanes like huge cow udders, edged with ruffles and flounces.

She wanted desperately to go home. Yet at home she'd wanted desperately to be here. Or anywhere. How weird was that? Anyway, happy endings were a lie or a mistake, and from now on she, Linda, would devote herself to the truth.

Everything was so safe in Donna's house. It was like having the windows closed all the time. Everything Donna needed or ever would need was there. She opened the window and flopped down backwards on Donna's extra twin bed.

"Hey, guys."

"Hey, Linds. Look. I'm doing Crissy's toenails. Glitter blue."

"Yeah. Nice."

"Want me to do yours next?"

"Sure."

Linda sat on the edge of the bed and unlaced her boots. She pressed her lips together hard, making a thin, tight line as she stared down at the rose-colored, thick-piled carpet. The blood roared in her ears. Donna and Crissy were not like her in any way. How had she not known that last year? Her cheeks burned with an inner fire, the burden of knowing her difference, her separateness. She leaned forward, pulled her boots off, and rested her head in her hands, closing her eyes while the warmth still pulsed hard in her face, behind her eyes. Tonight she would try to stay, to keep everything just like always. But there would come a time very soon when she and Donna and Crissy would split up for good.

"Okay, Crissy. Now don't move for five minutes. Guys. Look what I got!" Donna was saying. "True romance. *Moonstruck*."

"*Moonstruck*! With Cher?" Linda exclaimed. "Barf! She looks like a walking Barbie doll. Spare me."

"You know what, Linda?" Donna said hotly. "You're lucky I invited you over at all. You never want to do anything fun anymore. You just slink around, feeling sorry for yourself."

Linda blushed. She's right, she thought. I'm not fun anymore. I don't care about pop divas or their collagen lips, big behinds, and silicone implants.

Why should I have to learn to shake my booty in order to be someone? No one can even see my booty in my overalls. And a leather jacket would be perfect for covering me up on top. I just might get one. Yes, I would look mysterious in work boots and a leather jacket. And maybe a tattoo somewhere. A labyrinth. Something spirally and dark.

"I said," Donna shouted in Linda's face, "do you want double cheese, too? Crissy and I already ordered, space case."

"Double cheese? No. I want broccoli, mushroom, and feta."

"Linda!" Crissy complained. "We always get double cheese with meatballs."

"But it's not a law. I mean, I don't have to, right?"

Linda smiled at Crissy, who rolled her eyes. "Can't you be normal? Just for one overnight?"

"No." Linda grinned. "It seems I can't."

Donna hung up the phone. "Linda, you are so weird this year."

•

Just as they'd finished eating pizza at the breakfast bar in the kitchen, the doorbell rang. Donna's mother went to answer it.

"Linda!" called Donna's mom. "Your father's here."

"He is? Uh-oh." Linda's heart sank.

"What do you think he wants?" Crissy asked. "Are you in trouble?"

"Oh, I bet it's our creepy upstairs neighbor, who saw me at the park the other day. It's nothing."

Linda slid off her stool and padded to the front door in her bare feet. She smiled innocently at her father. "Hi, Dad."

"You need to come home, little one. Nanë's orders."

"But why now? Can't it wait?"

He shrugged. Linda hurried to get her things, her cheeks hot with embarrassment. She said goodbye as quickly as possible, and they left.

She and her father walked more or less silently along the tree-lined streets north toward Seventy-sixth Street.

"I'm grounded for the weekend, right? Because of Mrs. Maloney?" Linda asked.

"Yes, I guess so."

"She called Ma?"

"Yes."

Linda sighed, utterly humiliated. It would have been one thing to leave Donna's sleepover on her own, but to be walked home by her dad any time before eleven o'clock at night was a total disgrace.

"Why does Ma yell at me so much?" she asked.

"She wants the best for you. She's had a hard life, and

she wants things to be better for you. She wasn't allowed to finish school, you know. Age thirteen was her last year. Imagine that."

"I know her life was hard. But that was a long time ago. In Albania, for Pete's sake. Things would be a lot better for me if she stopped yelling," Linda grumbled. "If she let me do what I want and not what she wants. Like what's wrong with going to the park? I like it down there. Better than staying walled up in a stupid apartment all the time."

"Hey! That's enough!" her father said sharply.

Linda stopped talking. Her dad's method of discipline was none at all, followed by one warning, followed by one quick, stinging swat. Getting dragged out of Donna's was enough humiliation for the moment. She didn't need a swat on the backside.

The streetlights were on and a fluttering cloud of moths flickered around each encircling glow. Walking under the trees was like walking through a tunnel filled with soft light. Linda thought of her camera and of taking a photograph, but didn't quite know how. Wouldn't she have to use the flash? Would the automatic setting take care of it? Maybe she could get a book on photography from the library and try taking some night scenes. Well, Ramón's family cleaning the cinema, that would be at night. Midnight.

As they approached their building, Linda's father put his hand on her shoulder and gave it a little squeeze. Linda glanced up at him gratefully, but he opened the door instead of smiling back at her, and she realized that her dad had just switched sides. She was on her own.

Her mother jumped up from the couch, where she'd been watching TV, and hurried to the door. "No shoes!" she said automatically, following the Albanian custom. "The floor is clean."

Linda and her father left their shoes at the door and put on slippers.

"So. I get a call from Mrs. Maloney." Linda's heart sank. "She saw you. Down at the park all alone, without permission. She thinks there's a young man down there. Someone you meet. That's it. You are grounded. All weekend. No more coming and going all over the place."

Crack! Her mother hit her across the face. Linda cried out in pain and put her hand to her cheek and ear.

"You and your little secrets. You think I'm stupid? I never learned past grade eight, so now you think you know more? What are you doing with that young man, anyway?"

"Nothing! I don't know what you're talking about." Linda was crying now. She wished she weren't, but she couldn't help it. I will not take this. I will say one true thing, she told herself. No matter what the consequences. "What do you care, anyway? You like Tina more than me."

"Tina? Tina is a good girl. A beautiful girl. Look at you. Your clothes. What are you thinking of, dressed like that? Go to your room. You're grounded for the weekend. No TV, no phone, no nothing. We're going to Coney Island, but you can stay here."

"Good!" yelled Linda. "Ask me if I care!"

Linda went into her bedroom and shut the door. She

put her backpack in the closet. She looked at her reddened cheek in the mirror. Her eyes narrowed in anger. At that moment she hated her mother. And Dad? He was no help at all. He didn't have the energy to argue with her mother. He just wanted peace and quiet when he came home from the loud noise of construction equipment—the drills, the sandblaster, the jackhammers. He spent all day, all year, chipping away at rocks.

14

LINDA, ENTRENCHED IN SULLENNESS, wore her baggy clothes and a large papier-mâché fish clipped to her hair to school on Monday.

Ramón leaned across the aisle. "Hey, I like your fish. It looks like fishes I've seen scuba-diving off Cuba. Fish like that swim in the reefs."

Linda smiled at him.

"Pass your family project outlines forward, please," said Miss Wesley. "I'll have them back to you soon. Open House is in two and a half weeks. The final projects will be posted on the wall for your parents to learn something about the other students in the class. I've done it before, and it's been wonderfully successful."

As she spoke, Miss Wesley was passing out a new grammar review worksheet. Boring! Miss Wesley seemed obsessed with grammar.

"Psst! Hey!" Ramón whispered. "Did you do my out-

line? I can't get in trouble again like I did with the paragraph."

"Yeah. Here."

"Careful! Buns sees everything. Pass it down low."

She hadn't done much work on Ramón's outline. It
just said that Linda would take photos of them at their
midnight job. She was afraid that if she made it too de-
tailed, Buns would know Ramón hadn't written it.

Linda read hers over once more before handing it in.

A Photo Gallery: My Mother's Scar

A. Using photographs of children in Albania and the
surrounding area, I will show the terrible conditions in
the Balkans in 1918, when my grandparents were growing up. *Source:* Lewis Hine in Europe.

B. Using photographs from when I was little, I will
show how poor we were in our mountain village. *Source:*
there are no photos of me when I was little, so I will use
some from books on the region to show the bad conditions
in Albania under Communism.

C. Using photographs from the present, I will show my
mother's face now and the mysterious scar, and I will con-
tinue to try to find out how it happened.

She passed the outline forward to Crissy, who immediately started to read it.

"Crissy! No! It's private."

"Oh. Sorry." Crissy folded it down the middle and
passed it along.

Linda laid her head down on the desk. Her mother would never tell her where she came from or how she got the scar. She would simply rage at Linda, hate her, drive her away. How would Linda ever manage to survive all the way through high school like this? Her future was a narrow black tunnel, a culvert, instead of an arching bridge leading west into the sunset of possibilities.

"Ramón? Are you chatting?" It was Miss Wesley's voice. "You have just a few minutes left. Have you even started the grammar sheet?"

"Huh? Oh. No."

Linda glanced at him questioningly. Now it was too late to start the worksheet. Now he'd missed another assignment. It had happened like this last year. He kept falling further and further behind. He saw Linda watching him, and he gave her a bedraggled smile.

"Those papers should be just about finished, everyone," repeated Buns of Steel. "Another two minutes."

Linda saw Ramón glance hopelessly at the clock. He picked up his pencil and stared at the first sentence.

Linda made a decision. She erased her name at the top of her paper.

"Ramón, here," she whispered. Quickly she passed him her paper. "Now give me yours. We'll switch names. Put your name on mine."

Linda bent her head and raced to finish the paper before it had to be handed in. She had gotten halfway through when Buns began to stalk up and down the rows collecting them.

"Not finished, Linda? Daydreaming again?" asked Buns.

Linda shrugged. "I guess so. Sorry."

"Finish it for homework. Put it on my desk by 7:43 tomorrow morning."

With that, the bell rang.

·

After school, Linda edged into the crowded, noisy hallway. As she inched her way forward, she decided that now she would go straight to the park and make sure Andrei had cleared out of the hideout for good, although it would have been much wiser to stop at home first. But there was no way she could go home and listen to her mom yell at her even for five minutes.

Anyway, if he wasn't already, Andrei would soon be gone. She'd make absolutely sure he left. It was her hideout. He could go somewhere else, someplace that had nothing to do with her or Ramón. Or Miguel.

Then she could even run away from home if she had to, and live by the side of the bay like a bum. Just she and her camera. That was all she needed besides a little food. Linda smiled to herself. Who needed parents? They were such a pain. She thought of her dad switching sides on her the other night. Grownups could never be truly trusted. They made such a big deal out of things. They got so upset all the time and then blamed kids for it. Forget that!

She slowly shuffled her way down the wide front flight of stairs. Mullaney Junior High School was built in two wings, which converged at a wide central staircase that most of the students used at the beginning and end of the day, causing massive traffic jams. If a fight broke out when the halls and stairs were this crowded, a lot of kids got hurt. No one said anything about it, though. It was just another thing you had to put up with because you were a kid. Today everyone was jammed together because police were standing outside the doors, patting down some older boys. Pulling them aside for questioning. Must be something about drugs.

Suddenly Linda realized that Ramón was next to her on the stairs. He smiled at her. She smiled back, then glanced at his T-shirt. So what if it was old and stretched out? Actually, there was a hole under one arm. What was Donna and Crissy's point? He wore an old Yankees T-shirt. So what? She felt a flush of anger. Donna and Crissy were truly snobbish about clothes.

"Hey, Ramón, you want to go with me to the hideout now? Just for a few minutes? Come on. I'm going to make Andrei leave."

He sighed. "Okay. But this is a big mistake. I think we should just wait for the whole thing to blow over. There's nothing we can do about it. It's Miguel's fault to begin with. I mean maybe he really did steal a thousand dollars from those guys. Remember the money in his boot?"

"Yeah. How much do you think he had?"

"No idea. But you know what? I think they get it gambling. Or lose it gambling. Maybe that bar he says he works at is a gambling place. That's what Nadia told me."

Linda stared at him. "It's not all about gambling, Ramón. You're kidding yourself if that's what you think.

Anyway, if he *is* gambling, that's probably how he lost that money."

They pressed through the double doors at the bottom of the staircase and stepped outside. They crossed the school yard to a less crowded area, partly shaded by some sumac trees on the other side of the fence. Linda plunked her backpack on the ground for a minute and brushed her hair back from her face, letting the fresh air cool the back of her neck.

Donna and Crissy ran up to her.

"There you are!" Donna shouted. "We were looking everywhere for you. Hey! Want to come over? You can tell us what happened with your mom the other night. At least tell us, were you grounded? Oh." She noticed Ramón by Linda's side. "Well, never mind. Call me later," she said.

"Call us, you mean, Donna," echoed Crissy. "Come on. Let's go get a Popsicle. See you, Linda."

"Yeah. See you."

Linda felt a pang as she watched the two girls walk away together. Donna and Crissy were going home to paint glitter on their nails again, but probably a different color. Jade green maybe.

Linda thought, the truth is that I don't have my best friends anymore. Not like last year. But now it doesn't hurt so much. She was determined to move on with her life. She crouched over her backpack for a few minutes and brushed her hair so Ramón wouldn't say anything. As she straightened up, she spotted someone who looked familiar.

"Whoa. Hey! Ramón, look!"

Across the street at the opposite corner she saw a man, a small man with dark curly hair, leaning against a mailbox, holding a can of soda. Her heart jumped with curiosity and anxiety. She moved closer and peered through the open diamond spaces in the chain link fence.

"Who is it? Is it the guy from the harbor?" Ramón asked.

"I think so."

She squinted. It was hard to be sure. But he was scanning the crowd of kids who'd just gotten out of school. And he had a kind of patience about what he was doing that made Linda frightened.

Was he here because of her? Was he a stalker? She watched him toss the can into the trash container at the street corner. And then she saw him casually hand something—a brown paper bag?—to an older kid as he began to walk away.

"Oh my God! Did you see that? I told you they weren't making money gambling," Linda called over her shoulder. She was already running, determined to catch Andrei and confront him. "I'll be right back."

"Linda! No! Don't!" Ramón shouted. "Stay out of it!"

But she couldn't. Andrei was hanging around her school yard, selling dope. Recklessly, she tore across the street, running directly in front of a speeding delivery truck, which screeched its brakes and blared its horn as it narrowly missed her.

"Hey! Where's the fire, kid?" the driver shouted at her. "You want to get yourself killed?"

"Oh, shut up," she muttered under her breath.

Andrei was headed west, away from the school, back toward Third Avenue. Linda ran faster, pounding down the sidewalk until she caught up with him.

"Hey, Andrei!"

He turned around, nervously looking up and down the street as he did so. Then he smiled.

"What, brave girl? You are here?"

"Yeah. And I saw you, selling dope. That's my school, you idiot."

He grabbed her arm. "Quiet. You go with friends now."

"No. I told you before. Get out of here. Or I'll call the police, I swear to God I will. I saw what you did, Andrei. So don't bother lying to me. I have a witness, too."

He looked at her carefully. "No. No police. No more selling. Just one time. Okay? No problem. Stopping. It's okay."

Stopping. Did he mean it, that he would stop? He looked so serious.

"Not just stopping. Get out of here. I mean it."

"Listen. I am no criminal. Please, miss."

"Yes, you are. You came here to sell drugs. Well, you're hurting people. You're hurting Ramón's family and the kids in my school. I should never, ever have helped you. You didn't just swim here from a boat, starving and freezing and getting cut. I'll bet one of Miguel's friends cut you up because you stole from them."

He turned sideways, facing the school.

"Well?" she shouted.

He put his finger to his lips, indicating she should stop making so much noise.

"Okay. Don't answer. I know the truth, Andrei, whether you admit it or not." In disgust, Linda turned and jogged back to the school yard.

"Did you see him hand something to that kid, Ramón?" she asked.

He nodded. "Yeah. Unfortunately."

"Listen, they're dealers, Ramón."

"Miguel wouldn't do that, sell to kids like that. If I see a chance to talk with him, I'll try. We should go."

"But Andrei admitted it. Actually, he didn't have to admit it. I saw him do it."

Linda picked up her pack, and they started walking.

Ramón asked, "Do you think, if we called, the cops would go and find him at the hideout?"

"I don't know. I told him to leave. I hope he goes to California or something."

"California?" Ramón laughed. "How about Hawaii?"

"Yeah. Someplace really far away."

"China."

"Yeah. The top of Mount Everest. In a big snow-storm." Now she was laughing, too.

"Hey, thanks for doing my outline. How did yours go?"

"I tried to ask my mom some questions and she yelled at me."

"Like she always does."

"Yeah. Maybe I can do a famous person instead. Get a

book from the library. My parents don't want me talking to anybody about where we came from and how we got here."

"So, there's only one reason for that. 'Cause you're illegal, right?"

Linda looked away. "Yeah. I guess."

"Hey, Linda, I know you are." Ramón took her arm and looked seriously into her eyes. "But it's not your fault. Don't worry. I won't tell."

He gave her a quick hug. They headed toward her street in silence.

"How did you know?" she asked finally.

"I just know."

"Are you?" she asked.

"What?"

"Are you illegal?"

"No. My mother didn't have much trouble going for the visa. We waited for it only six months. I think there is a special lottery for Cuba so people don't cross to Florida in boats."

"Oh. You know what? I keep having nightmares," Linda finally said. "This year is starting off so bad. I dream about Andrei, clinging to a barrel in the gray water, only then it turns out to be me, and I'm drowning. I keep swallowing water and choking. It's so awful. So that stinks. And I just don't feel close to Donna and Crissy anymore. I'm going to dump them. Then I won't have any friends at all."

"I don't have any friends at all either. Except you."

Linda nodded, glancing at his face. His deep brown eyes and brown skin reflected glints of late afternoon sunlight. She smiled.

"School can be awful," Ramón said. "It is for me. Hey, listen. You like coffee?"

"No," Linda said, laughing. "Actually, I hate it."

"Well, too bad. Come on. Let's go to Geppetto's. We won't stay long. I go there with Nadia at night, when she wants to go out. It's fun. There's music."

"Okay."

"You can't live without music, right?"

"My mom never listens to music. They weren't allowed to in her country. You know what I like?" Linda said.

"No, what?"

"I like September because of the way the light falls on things. I feel like I'm swimming in light," Linda said.

Now, suddenly, she was caught in a kaleidoscope of good and bad moments, of glowing colors and inky black spots, exhilarating yet scary. Was she going crazy, or was this normal for eighth graders? She had no idea.

"You mean 'cause it's warm and glowing and it sort of holds you?" Ramón asked.

"Yeah."

"Yeah? That's yellow, I think. It's a great color, especially if you mix it with others. Well, music's like that, too. It surrounds you and holds you up. Keeps you going."

"I don't really know a lot about music," Linda said.

"No! Are you kidding me? Everyone in Cuba loves music. Where was it your parents came from again?"

"Albania."

"I never heard of it."

"Nobody has. It's near Greece." Near Greece. Now she couldn't help thinking about Andrei again. But she wouldn't let him ruin this moment.

Ramón opened the door and they stepped inside. Geppetto's was air-conditioned, and the coolness felt good after a hot day in school. They went to a small table in the back so that Ramón could sit near the speakers. Some soft jazz was playing in the background. Large, colorful abstract paintings hung on the walls.

"Listen," Ramón said. He closed his eyes. "Is this great, or what?"

Linda closed her eyes, too. He was right. The sound did surround her and soothe her.

"It feels like having your hair brushed over and over," she said.

"My hair is one inch long, so I wouldn't know," Ramón said. "Now we have to order. If you hate coffee, get cappuccino like me."

When the two cappuccinos arrived, they looked like hot chocolate with a sprinkle of cinnamon and chocolate on top of froth, all floating on the surface.

"Now put a ton of sugar in it," Ramón advised.

Linda dumped sugar in her cup and stirred. Some froth spilled over the side.

"I wish I had an older sister."

"You *are* an older sister."

"Yeah." Linda felt a sharp pang of guilt over the irritable way she treated Tina. She snapped at Tina just the way her mother snapped at her. "I'm not very nice to Tina."

"Well, you should be," Ramón said. "No matter how dumb she acts. She's little, you know?"

Linda nodded.

"None of what's wrong for you is her fault."

"Yeah, I know."

"So if you yell at her, it's just like your mom yelling at you. Maybe worse, 'cause you're not doing it for her good."

Linda thought for a moment. "Okay, okay. I get it."

He smiled at her. "So this is cool here, right?"

She smiled back. "Very."

After a moment Linda said, "You know what I'd like? The school recommended me for this special program at Clemens Academy. I'd really like to go there. You can study whatever you want and even take college classes and have a mentor to help you decide stuff. Like I could take a class in social justice. Like how unjust is immigration, did you ever think of that? And there's photography! No worksheets! Freedom from worksheets! Doesn't it sound great?"

"Yeah, it does. Not great for me. But for you. So what's the problem? Your mom won't let you?"

"No." She stirred the thick mound of froth on her cappuccino.

Tears of disappointment welled in Linda's eyes, but for once they were calm tears, not hot, angry ones. If she really wanted to try the Clemens place, she'd have to keep telling her teachers. Especially Miss Wesley. Show them how much an opportunity like that would mean to her.

They sipped their cappuccinos, not talking much after that. And it was peaceful, just hanging out quietly. Linda let out a big sigh and felt her shoulders relax. This kind of understanding was something she had to have to be her real self. Perhaps it wasn't really to be found by escaping to a beat-up old hideout. Perhaps she needed to be among other people and quietly stake her claim there and wait and see what happened.

Half an hour later, as she neared her home, the sunny yellow mood she'd had when she'd been with Ramón faded, and she began to feel anxious again—the heart-pounding-too-hard feeling. It was thoughts of her mother that did it. Keep moving, she told herself. If necessary, sing. Maybe the meatball song again. Softly, now. "On top of spaghetti, all covered with cheese, I lost my poor meat-ball when somebody sneezed."

Linda headed west on Seventy-sixth. The afternoon air was soft and laden with sulfurous pollution that stained the edges of the sky light brown.

Linda frowned, full of doubts now about what she was going to do. Was she wrong? It was beautiful and peaceful by the water; maybe that's why Andrei wanted to stay. Maybe he and Miguel were just friends. Maybe they sold dope only once. Maybe she shouldn't be so suspicious about things she really knew nothing about. If she did call the police, and didn't give her name, maybe they could trace the call and would come find her. And what if her parents truly were illegal—and it seemed they had to be—would the police make them all leave the country? Except Tina? Was that why her mother was afraid of the police?

Maybe—this seemed like her only choice—if she threatened Andrei enough, he'd be gone by tomorrow and things at Ramón's house would return to normal. That would be great! But when should she sneak down there? This afternoon? Should she? Or shouldn't she? Now that she was nearly home, she felt a little hungry. They hadn't eaten anything at Geppetto's. A snack would be nice.

When she reached the entryway to her apartment, she sat down on the cement wall. The ground was wet where her mother had rinsed everything off with the hose. She was going to take a photo of her mother doing that. And she'd take the photo from a certain angle so the long snaky-thin scar would show, pointing the way like a lightning bolt. She'd talk to her mom first. Andrei would have to wait.

15

AFTER WASHING THE SUPPER DISHES and taking the trash out to the numbered garbage cans (theirs was can number 1A), Linda went into her bedroom and closed the door. She swept a pile of Barbie clothes from her bed and dumped them on Tina's, then patted her quilt to see if all was clear. She hated sitting down on plastic Barbie shoes with the spike heels. Those things could hurt! First she checked her camera. Fifteen more shots on this roll. ASA 400. No problem there.

She opened her backpack and took out her books, flipping idly through her social studies chapter. But her thoughts strayed to the family history project. Where had they come from? And how? That was the Big Secret in this house.

"Ma!" she hollered, tossing her book aside. She wasn't going to back down this time. She'd confronted Andrei once. Now for Ma.

She went into the living room. Her father still wasn't home from work. Sometimes on warm nights, the crew stayed late to make up for hours lost in the winter. Her mother was watching television, an all-news talk show that she couldn't possibly understand.

"Ma, listen, please? I have to do a project for English, remember I told you already? About us, where we came from. So, since we don't have any old photos, you'll have to tell me—"

"Have to tell you nothing. Now, out. I'm watching something."

"But I'll flunk. Miss Wesley is a hard teacher. She grades hard."

"Okay. Write something nice. Something pretty. Be nice for a change. Your teacher will be happy."

Linda frowned in disgust. Something pretty? A nice lie, that was what she meant. Linda went into the kitchen and scooped some vanilla pudding into a bowl.

Tina pranced in. "I want some, too," she said.

Remembering Ramón's comments, Linda smiled at her sister and handed her a bowl. There, she told herself, that didn't hurt too much. She wandered back to her room and opened her social studies book. She read ten pages and started the chapter review questions. All she had to do to answer them was go back and find the right caption under the right picture, but that was copying out of the book. She was supposed to think of something interesting to say, not paraphrase captions. But thinking of interesting comments was hard. After five questions, she let the book fall to the floor, her mind numb.

Linda lay down and pulled the blanket over her head, and suddenly she was sound asleep, a strange, early evening sleep, where noises grew in dreams like house plants reaching out for the walls, the woodwork, grasping for places to attach to.

It was dark. There were a lot of people, tall, whispering, shadowy people. She couldn't understand what they said. And then red taillights from cars. Her mother got in the little space, tucked up against the wall of the car trunk as tight as possible. Linda climbed in. She was so little that she could fit snugly up against her mother. At first it was fun being there, but then it got scary.

Linda wanted to get out. Her mother had promised they would be in the trunk only a little while. There were guns. Someone else climbed into the little space. A man's big shoes were pressed against her face. Two men were arguing about her. One tried to pull her out of the car. They didn't want children in there. Now the trunk was closed and it was hot. And she had to be absolutely quiet. The car wasn't going. It was so hot. There was no air.

"We're going to die in here," the man whispered.

She wanted to cry. She was crying. Her mother stuffed a sock in her mouth. Linda was choking, dying, like the harbor man. No police. Not ever. No police.

Abruptly awake, Linda sat up, sweaty and breathing fast. She was still in her bedroom. Tina was getting into her pajamas and the bedroom door was open. The seashell nightlight was on. Tina had already had her bath. She padded over to Linda in bare feet.

"Are you hot? You look all sweaty. Are you sick?" Tina asked.

"No. I'm okay."

Linda went slowly down the hall into the bathroom. She got a washcloth and rinsed it with cool water, then sponged off her forehead.

She'd had the dream before, but never so vividly, with so much detail. Even now that she was awake, it felt so real. She couldn't go back to sleep. Not right now. Was this more hormone hell? Maybe she should slice up a cucumber and put the slices on her eyelids.

Her father had gotten home. He came into the hall.

"Well, look who's up. Is school wearing you out already? Look at you. You're all sweaty. How about some ice cream?"

Her mother came into the hall, too.

"What's wrong? Are you sick? Why are you sleeping so early?"

"Nothing's wrong! I'm fine. Really."

"I'm getting you some ice cream. You need something cool," her dad said as he left. "You want vanilla? Maple walnut?"

"Yeah. Not vanilla. Maple walnut."

Linda went into the living room and turned off the TV. The noise and bright colors bothered her.

"Your father was watching that," her mother said.

"Ma, please. How did we get here? You and me? We came in the trunk of a car, right?"

Her mother's face froze. She got a guarded, cautious look and, instead of answering, flicked two imaginary specks of dust off the gleaming surface of the coffee table. She rearranged the pink plastic flowers in their vase.

"Leave them, Ma. Tell me. Please."

"Why? Why do you have to know this? Because of that teacher? That family project?"

"No. It's not just her. I don't know why," Linda whispered. "I just do."

"All right," her mother said. "After we crossed the river from Mexico, we came north in the trunk of a car. There were three of us in that trunk, and we all nearly died. It was so hot. So hot. You can't imagine. We got a ride from the Texas side, near El Paso, up into New Mexico. Six thousand dollars I paid for that car ride and we almost didn't make it. For three years your father sent me money. To northern Greece. I had you in Greece. Never would I have another child in Albania. I kept you in Greece. In the mountains. Then we came here."

Greece? She came from the same place as Andrei.

"But, I mean, another child? Besides me and Tina?" Linda said, puzzled.

"Yes. I had a baby boy in Albania, but he died there. I swore never to have another child there."

"So how did we get from Greece to Mexico?" Linda asked. "By boat?"

"No. We flew from Athens, Greece, to Mexico City with an illegal passport. Then we went north in a truck with a Polish man. The plan was that the Mexicans on that side of the border would drop us off at the river. On the other side of the river is America.

"Where we were, they told us the Rio Grande is very shallow and they told us not to worry, there is even a gravel bar in the middle, so we won't have to swim. The banks are lined with heavy, tall grass full of winding paths that aliens have taken during their escapes.

"Then, on the other side, we would have to run through farm ranches and barbed wire to the highway, where a car would meet us and drive us six hours farther north, away from the highway checkpoints in Texas and New Mexico.

"You know," she said, "you and I are a lot alike."

No. I don't want to hear this. I don't want to know this, Linda thought. I will never be like you. Never.

Her mother smiled. "You and I—we are what they say here, 'bad news.'

"Anyway. The searchlight was like a big broom, sweeping light over everything. We had to duck our heads down in the water when it came past. But you didn't understand.

I had to put your head under. You kicked me and fought. So I had to pinch your nose and duck you under. And then you would try to scream and your mouth would fill up with water. Oh God. It was awful."

"I think I remember," said Linda. "I thought I was drowning. I still have nightmares about this."

"Yes, probably," said her mother. "You kicked and fought me and twisted in my arms. The Mexicans had lied to us. Out in the middle of the river, there was no gravel bar. It was deep, chest-deep, and there was a strong current. One thousand people drown in that river every year, trying to cross. You twisted and wriggled in my arms like a little eel. I could barely hold you. And then suddenly you broke free, dropping down into the black water like a stone. Then I cried out for help. The man who had been in the truck with us, the Polish man, came back and dived under the surface and pulled you up, then helped me hurry the rest of the way.

"By now we were terrified about whether we'd make it. We could be sent to jail; our money for bribes could be stolen. Anything could happen. The closer we got to freedom, the more frightened we became. We climbed out of the water and scurried along the bank like rats. A border runner was waiting for us. We crossed a ranch and the rancher came out, turning on all his lights and yelling and waving a rifle at us. But we never stopped running.

"The border runner brought us to the car. There we had to give the rest of our money for the driver to take us around all the highway checkpoints. We were driven in the trunk of a car six hours north of El Paso, many times not on highways but on rough land, banging us and bruising us. As the sun came up, it was so hot. And there was no air.

"The three of us were crammed in that trunk, the Polish man, me, and you. I had stuffed a sock in your mouth so you couldn't cry. I cried to myself in silence because I was afraid you might suffocate.

"The Polish man went to Chicago. I wanted to thank him for his help, but I couldn't. I always wanted to write to him. I think of him even today."

Linda didn't say anything.

"I wanted you to grow up in freedom," her mother added.

Linda sat quietly, thinking about how brave and fierce her mother was, how she had risked her life for Linda to bring her here to this place, to this country of the some free/some not, the home of the brave, the country of almost justice. The brave part was true because of her mother and father, but the justice? It was hard to know, for if America was truly just, why would a child like her be excluded from belonging?

"We're never going back?" Linda asked finally.

"No," her mother answered. "We can't get a passport. I can never see my parents again, even if they are dying. You will never see your grandparents. We must stay here and try for a better life."

"Can we ever become legal?" Linda wondered.

"No. I don't know, but I don't believe so. Don't think about it. And don't talk about this anymore."

"But I have to think about it. It's my life. Am I illegal for my life? Ma, what am I? What nationality?"

Her mother shrugged. "Does it matter? You're here."

"Yes, it matters more than anything," Linda said. "Tell me."

"All right, then. You're Albanian."

But I want to be American, she thought. The truth is that the place you are born is your fate, your history, set in cement. Stone. Even so, her mother had tried to change that. Fighting like a lioness for Linda so she could be free.

Then her dad came with the ice cream, and after that it was too late to take photos of her mom—and much too late to go talk to Andrei. She'd have to ask about the scar another time. She had enough to think about for now.

16

On Tuesday morning, Miss Wesley handed back the paragraphs and outlines. "MacGregor," she called out, holding both of Crissy's papers aloft.

Crissy darted up to get them, then sashayed back to her seat. As soon as she sat down, she turned to Linda. "Ha, ha. My outline has the Buns of Steel stamp of approval." She waved her outline in front of Linda's face.

"Ahhh," said Linda. "Thanks for the nice, cool breeze."

"Berati." Miss Wesley's voice rang out.

Linda hurried up for her papers and went back to her seat. The outline had a red check-plus on the top. But the topic paper had a large *See me* scrawled across it. She quickly folded it in half.

"I'm going to focus on women in my family and, like, the medical profession, because my mom's a nurse," Crissy said. "What about you?"

"Oh, I don't know," Linda said, suddenly self-conscious. "Something to do with photography. A portrait or something."

"Yeah? Let me see your paragraph."

Shrugging, Linda handed Crissy the folded paper.

"Whoa. 'See me'? Wait a sec." Crissy read it, frowning, then handed it back. "You shouldn't have mentioned how wacked your mother is. I bet Buns is going to zero in on that when she talks to you."

"I just wanted to write something that I really thought and felt."

"Well, good luck. Let me know how it goes when you talk with Buns. I hope you're not in trouble or anything."

Crissy, Linda decided, was much, much nicer than Donna. Maybe someday she and Crissy could become good friends if Donna moved on to boys for good. That might work.

"Okay, class, read the first short story in the text," said Miss Wesley. "I want to talk to a few of you individually. Ramón Nieves? Up here, please."

Linda glanced sharply at him. Uh-oh.

When Ramón returned to his seat, he didn't look at her. He just pointed his finger at the story and started to wade through it.

Finally the bell rang, signaling the end of first period.

"Linda? Up front."

"Good luck," Ramón whispered.

Linda sighed and dragged her backpack up to the teacher's desk. Miss Wesley was noting some information in her planning book while the class filed out for second period.

Miss Wesley looked up and smiled. "I liked what you wrote about your mother."

"You did?"

"Yes, although I think you could push it a lot further. Especially with that surprising history of the region you uncovered with the Lewis Hine book."

"Oh." Linda nervously wondered where this conversation might be heading.

"Linda, I appreciate your attempts to help Ramón. I am fully aware that he needs help, though, and that's what I'm here for. It's fine with me if you take photos for Ramón, but you are not, I repeat, *not*, to write one word of the captions. And no more help with his worksheets. Ramón needs to get involved. He can't sit there and doodle his life away."

"But what if he fails?" she asked, blushing.

"He will certainly fail if he doesn't try. And you can both fail if you cheat. You're in here to concentrate on your own work and to develop your own skills. This makes me even more determined not to let you off the hook about transferring to Clemens. That program is designed for free spirits like you."

A free spirit? Is that what she was, then? There was a name for the oddness she felt?

"You know," Miss Wesley continued, "I never heard back from your mother after my phone call. Did you give her the message?"

"Yes," Linda said softly.

Miss Wesley tapped her pencil eraser on her attendance book. "Is something going on at home, Linda? Is there a problem?"

"No, no. Everything's okay. Really!"

"There's nothing you want to tell me about? Are you in over your head with something?"

How could Miss Wesley guess such a thing? She *was* in over her head. With Andrei. With Miguel. But how could she tell a teacher what was happening?

"I think I can manage for now. But it's just . . . about the Clemens program? My mom didn't call because she simply said no. Flat-out no. My mom's great; she's really brave and stuff, but she never listens to me. So could you . . . I mean, I'd really, really like to go to Clemens. Could you not give up on my mom? Could you keep trying to reach her and persuade her to let me go?"

Linda's heart was pounding. It was the first time she'd ever talked to a teacher this way. And Miss Wesley of all people!

"I won't give up. I can be pretty stubborn, too. Now you go on."

After school, the girls wandered over to the fence.

"Hey," Crissy said. "I forgot to ask you at lunch. What did Buns say when she kept you after class?"

"Nothing."

"I hope you didn't tell her anything personal."

"No. It went okay." Linda didn't want to talk about it.

"Let's go over to my house," Donna said. "You never told us what happened the other night when your dad came for you, either."

"I got grounded. You know my mom. I don't think I'll come over. I have some things to do."

"Like what?" Donna asked.

"Oh, chores and stuff. Watching Tina."

"It doesn't seem like you want to hang out with us anymore," Crissy said.

"I'm just busy. Okay?"

"Yeah? Busy with Ramón? Busy with that homeless guy?" Donna teased.

"Watch it," Linda said.

"Well, what about Friday, then? I'm having another sleepover. Just you and Crissy. And then the next week, we can have it at Crissy's."

"I'll try. But don't count on me coming."

"You better try," said Donna. "We can't have you hanging out with Ramón all year."

"Why not? He's a really good friend. It bothers me how you guys treat him. You're such snobs," said Linda hotly.

"Whatever," said Donna, laughing. "Come on, Crissy."

The two girls wandered across the street to the corner store. Moments later, they came out with ice cream bars. They stood at the trash container on the corner and peeled off the paper wrappers, then headed down the street to Donna's.

Linda watched while a bag lady came to the trash container where Donna and Crissy had just tossed their wrappers. Like other homeless people Linda had noticed, she wore a heavy winter coat bound around the waist with ropes. That was probably because she didn't want to lose the coat and it was better to tie it on, no matter what the weather. Just like the thousands of Balkan children in the Lewis Hine photographs. Their coats were tied to them.

The lady set down her shopping bags and pawed through the trash, looking for cans. Linda could just imagine what Donna might whisper to Crissy about the bag lady.

And suddenly, through light years of loneliness, Linda felt a gleaming pinpoint, a sudden ray of knowing. As she watched the lady poke through the mounds of dirty paper in the trash container, an idea started to form about the photographs she wanted to take for her social studies project. With a camera, she could send out a beam of light, of recognition, to hold things in their place for a moment before letting them go. Like picking up a single shell at the beach out of thousands and holding it in your palm, turning it over and over to see how it was formed, and then showing it to someone else.

Linda knew she should go to the hideout and see if Andrei was there. But that could take time, and her mother might worry.

On the way home, she stopped at the branch library to get a book on photography. She was completely absorbed, looking at all the photography books, and when she glanced at the clock, she was startled to see it was after four. She checked out a book about darkrooms and one on digital imagery and hurried for the door.

•

"Again, where are you? Huh? Look at the time!"

"Ma, please. I was at the library. I have a report due in a week, I told you."

"Library. Always the library. Donna called. About the sleepover this Friday."

"What? I already told her I couldn't come. What did she call for? I have to go help Ramón with his—"

"Ramón?" Her mother's voice became higher, louder, more and more out of control. "Not go to Donna's? You should be with Donna. Her nice family. Running off with that Ramón all the time, when I told you not to? You think you can keep secrets from me? After what I did for you, to bring you here?"

"What was the big deal?"

Slap! Her mother's hand flew out, cracking Linda across her cheek.

"Never mind. You are right. I did what I had to do. That's all," her mother hissed, pushing her into her room. "Now, stay out of my sight."

Linda felt something inside her head snap. Pure rage blinded her.

"Yeah? Well, you keep secrets from everybody. Just tell me how you got that stupid scar. Stop lying."

The sentence flew out of Linda's mouth. Her mother raced forward and seized her arm, and pushed her forcibly into her bedroom and slammed the door. Linda ran to the bed and lay down and cried.

Who are the grandparents I can never meet? And where is my brother buried? Is that why Ma's angry? Because she left so much behind to get me out of there?

She had to stand alone, rigid, cut off from her past by her mother's force of will. Told not to find out, to become proud of beauty pageants, to never raise her voice, to wear white Sunday school–type clothes. And mostly to be happy and grateful—for water in the faucet, for air to breathe. No matter how well she was doing, how happy she was, it was never enough. She had to make up for all of Communism. For the scar, for her lost brother. It was crazy. And it wasn't the trip through Mexico that made her mother angry like this. There was still something Linda didn't know.

Wiping away her tears, she opened the Lewis Hine book of photographs. She stared at a photograph of a Greek shepherd girl standing all alone on a steep, treeless hillside. Was that like the place where she had been born? How did it feel, she wondered, to be in that place with just the hills and the sky, while all around you there was war after war, and later Nazis invading. And then, after the Nazis left, came the Communist dictators.

Suddenly her mother came in. Linda sat up and slammed the Lewis Hine book closed.

"You will obey me about this. No more being late from school. You will listen to me! This is a dangerous world. You can get yourself in a lot of trouble if you're not careful. See? You don't believe me. And what do you know? Nothing. But I grew up under Communism. Under a dictator. I lived in stones, in dirt. I got this on my face, this scar. 'Ma, tell me what happened,' you say. How can you understand my life? You can't. It's best to forget. Do you hear?"

Linda was crying openly now. But her mother went on.

"It's not their business, any of this, at the school. Family project. The family is private; it's not for them to know. It's like under Communism, spies everywhere, at your own dinner table, outside under the window. And why do you need this?"

She grabbed hold of the camera strap, but Linda pulled it away from her. "No! Ma! Stop it! I have to take photos of you and then some of Ramón and his family working at the cinema at midnight. I told you. For his family project. It's not my fault they work at night. And I want to take pictures of our life here, of you, since we don't have any old ones. That's going to be my project."

Her mother sat on the edge of Tina's bed and rubbed her forehead. Linda waited. Several minutes passed before her mother spoke again. "Of me? No."

"That's not fair. You want me to be like other kids, but you don't act at all like other moms. Ramón's mother's nice. Donna's mother is nice. But you yell at me all the time. And I hate it!"

Her mother stared at the floor, not moving. Linda waited, hardly breathing.

"All right. All right. I see now you have to do this

project in school. Do your work, then. Take my picture. I don't care. Go at two in the morning to clean this cinema like a peasant, like a nobody. Show everybody my scar."

Immediately, Linda began to think about the pictures she would make. Tina standing on the polished walnut coffee table in her frilly socks, their dad tired and dusty at the end of the day, Ma hosing down the walkway in her flowered housedress and flip-flops. Ma sewing, the sewing machine light tracing the curve of the scar down her chin. She would put a story under each photo, little stories like the one Ramón had told her, about the boom of the cannon in Havana harbor and about the music at Geppetto's.

"Now I have to finish that dress," her mother murmured, and left the room.

Who cut you, Ma? Who cut your face from below your eye to under your chin? Linda said in her mind. That was the next step. The answer to that.

It hadn't happened. But it had to. Right now.

Linda got up and walked to the door, her heart pounding. It wasn't locked. She could open it. She would pretend to be a princess, awakened after years of sleep. She had to rescue her mother, who was under an evil spell. And it wasn't Tina who could free her. It was Linda, the one and only. Linda the Magnificent with her camera, the magic wand that showed life truthfully, all revealed in the glowing red cave of the darkroom.

She went into her parents' bedroom, where her mother was sewing a dress. Linda drew herself up to her full height. She put her eye to the viewfinder and framed her mother's sitting figure, the drape of the dress on her lap, the squint of her eyes, the glint of the gold thimble, the flash of the splendidly silver needle, and the pale scar that followed the contour of her cheek and jaw. Linda took her mother's picture.

"Mom," she said, "never mind the school project for now. I'm thirteen years old. I need to know how you got that scar."

Her mother stopped sewing. She put aside the dress and sighed. For once, she didn't yell.

17

"ALL RIGHT, THEN.

"The story started years ago, with my uncle, when he was eighteen, and with me, your mother, still not born yet. My parents lived in a little town in the Pindus Mountains on the Albanian side of the border. In that region, the steep, rocky mountains are very high, like Alps, and covered with snow from time to time. They separate Albania from Greece. And for centuries there were terrible wars all over this place.

"Then came the Albanian Communists with their secret police. Even if the people wanted to resist this regime, they couldn't. What did we have that was ours? A few stones? A tired donkey who had to be hit with sticks to make him walk? Everyone was so poor."

Her mother laid the dress on top of the sewing machine and went to her bag of yarn and knitting needles. She reached in and took out a ball of blue wool. The wool was all crinkled because she had taken it, raveled, from a wool sweater that Linda had outgrown. Her hands always had to be busy.

"I'll use this wool over. Make you some warm socks for winter, all right?" her mother said. "Now. Hold on a minute. I have to count this first row."

Linda watched her mother's lips move silently as she cast on the knitting stitches. She started the second row.

"Ma," Linda reminded her.

"All right. In Albania, under our dictator, the secret police were everywhere, listening and watching, spying on people's every move in case anyone tried to escape. Devil people. If one person escaped, they would find the rest of the family and put them into a labor camp. All of them—mother, father, babies. Whole families were put into these camps.

"My youngest uncle ran away when he turned eighteen, so we were all arrested. The secret police came for us. My mother was pregnant with me. We were forced into the back of an old truck and driven ten hours through the mountains to the plains, the swamps. We were put into a forced labor camp.

"We were assigned a two-room apartment for grandparents, parents, children. It had a tiny kitchen, a sitting room, and one bedroom. There was one bed. When my mother went to turn on the water, no water ran from the faucet. And it did not run the next day, or the next . . .

"On the second day, my parents were told to report to the cornfields before dawn. But first they had to walk two miles to the camp office to register. So they got up at four in the morning to do this. There were many other people, families, walking through the gray dawn, but no one spoke, not even the children.

"My mother was handed a pickax to break up clods of dirt. My grandmother was given a shovel. She was seventy years old. And they started to work in the cornfields. For the next twelve hours, they had to dig.

"And so we lived like this. One loaf of bread and never enough water. My family was sentenced to fifteen years because of the escape of my uncle. And I, who wasn't even born yet, I was, too.

"After I was born, my grandmother watched me while my mother worked in the fields—digging potatoes, wheat, cotton, fruit, corn. And all the food was packed and shipped away. We never got to eat it. We were given only bread and more bread. We were always bitterly hungry and half-mad with thirst. We went barefoot all the time.

"It was the job of us little ones, under age seven, to watch for the water tank towed by a tractor. It came every few days, but we never knew when, or how much water it would bring. In any case, there was never enough. We had to be quick and strong to get any at all.

"One day, while I was playing in the dirt outside our apartment, I saw the water tank coming. I ran inside for the jars. So did every other child. And then we all ran madly, scrambling, clawing our way past the others, for the tractor. But on this day, while running as fast as I could, I tripped in the middle of the road. I fell.

"One of the jars broke and cut my face, chin, and neck deeply. I remember lying in the road on my back, screaming, terrified from seeing all the blood, and my grandmother coming. Someone fetched my father. None of the families had a car. So my father got a bicycle and sat me sideways on the crossbar in front of him. He told me to cling to his waist. There was a doctor in Lushnja five miles away.

"The doctor tried to stitch me up, but he had no anesthesia, just needle and thread, and I screamed and fought like a little animal, so he gave up. The bleeding had stopped by then anyhow.

"So," said Linda's mother, bending to her knitting. "Now I've told you about how I got my scar.

"After age thirteen, children in the camps weren't allowed to go to school anymore."

"At my age?"

"Yes. I had to work in the field twelve hours a day.

"Finally our dictator died. The whole Communist regime collapsed, and the country went into absolute chaos. Riots. Burning. Looting. My family was released from the labor camp. They gave us about two dollars. But after all that time, we had no idea where to go, what to do. Should we go back to Korce? The Communists had declared us enemies of the people and taken our land years ago. There was no hope of getting it back. The secret police who had once destroyed our lives were still very much in power, officially and unofficially.

"Life in Korce was terrible. There wasn't enough to eat. People stole everything you can imagine. Wires out of hospital walls. Water pipes under the street. Panes of glass. Fruit trees were cut down and burned as firewood. Your older brother died in the maternity hospital because we didn't have bribe money to get a doctor to help him. That was it. That was it!"

Her mother's voice rose in near hysteria.

"I swore then I would leave. I made your father go first, even though I was already pregnant again. He escaped to Italy and then to America. He wanted me to wait with my parents until he was settled. But they seemed so old. So tired out. And me hungry and pregnant! Do you like hearing this, Linda? How I abandoned my elderly parents to save you? I will never see them again. After what we went through."

Linda was crying, but she didn't move. She didn't stop her mother.

"So I didn't tell them. I knew they would go crazy and try to stop me. One night I left secretly. I walked through the mountains, in the snow. Into Greece. I stayed there three years in a little farmhouse. With the best people in the world. You were born there. In a tiny herding village in Epirus. And when your father sent enough money, we left."

"And we crossed the Rio Grande and came here," Linda said.

"That's right."

Tina entered the living room, dragging her Barbie clothes case and dream house with her. "What?" Tina asked. "What were you telling Linda?"

"Never mind, Miss Big Ears," her mother said. "When you're older, I'll tell you, too. Not now."

Linda smiled at Tina. "Come on, Tina Banana. I'll play Barbies with you. But only for five minutes! And they aren't really Barbies; they are monsters in disguise. Let's play in our room. I get to have the red-haired Barbie. She's actually an ogress with eyes of fire."

Tina gave a squeal of excitement and skipped ahead down the hall to their room. Linda lay on the floor while redheaded Barbie hid under the bed. Black-haired Barbie was in an evening gown.

After months and months of arguing with her little sister (she remembered Ramón's comment that she was an older sister like Nadia), she felt that she owed Tina a little time. Besides, hearing the truth from her mother made her feel closer to her family. So she stayed where she was, and when black-haired Barbie came prancing along on her clear plastic spike heels, ogress Barbie rushed from her cave, roaring, and pounced on her, dragging her off by her hair.

18

WEDNESDAY MORNING, Linda sat in homeroom with her head on her desk, staring sideways at Ramón, who was drawing an elaborate battleship surrounded by helicopters. He didn't glance her way, and she wondered why not. She'd brought her camera to school, but now felt self-conscious about using it. Before first period began, Miss Wesley called Linda up front again.

"Uh-oh, Linda," Crissy whispered. "Buns alert. She's got you in her sights now."

"Shut up, Crissy," said Linda tiredly. She approached the teacher's desk.

Buns held up two rolls of high-speed film. "Remember, you can take the photographs, but the written part of his project is up to Ramón. No cheating!"

So, Linda thought, now, on top of everything else, I'm still a cheat. A liar. A sneak. And aiding a man I thought was a stowaway—probably that was a crime, too.

Wow. Teen girl chooses life of crime. But Buns was right. It was up to her, not Linda, to help Ramón. Was Miss Wesley mad at her or not? She'd given Linda film!

She dropped the film into the pockets of her overalls. Then, after English class, Linda pressed her cheek against the coolness of the cinderblock wall in the crowded hallway and reached into her pockets. The film felt like small rolls of gold, like coins that she wanted to spend right away.

The crush of kids kept pushing past her until the hall was empty. Then she set off for social studies, twirling in slow circles as she walked. Never be normal, never be normal, she chanted under her breath. Not being normal was very easy. Stop lying. Stop lying. That was harder.

She wouldn't go straight home today, she decided. Today would be the big day. She'd put it off long enough. She would go down to the hideout. With luck, Andrei would be long gone. And then she could lie in the grass and take a break. Get away from everyone. As long as she kept a sharp lookout for Mrs. Maloney on the way home, she should be okay. And if she did run into her, well, the light in the afternoon filtering through the plane trees, so soft and hazy, that would be just perfect for photos.

"Hey, Mr. Belisle."

"Morning, Linda. Not going to make late arrivals a habit, are we?"

"Nope. Sorry."

"Take your seat, dude."

Another period; another world. Teachers were so different from one another.

.

At three-fifteen, Linda and Ramón wandered down Seventy-third Street. Brooklyn smelled different there. Metal trapdoors were open in the sidewalk so deliveries could be stored in the shop basements. The cool damp air blew up from the dark holes.

Cardboard boxes littered the streets once their merchandise was emptied. Strips of shredded white packing paper blew about the sidewalk like paper spaghetti. These she photographed. Oddly shaped crumpled paper that had once held eggplants, yellow onions, and chives drifted away on the afternoon breeze, heading for the bay like ground-level kites.

"So did you ask Miguel what the deal was with him and Andrei?" Linda asked.

"Oh. No. I couldn't. He and my mom have been fighting so much. About those two guys and the money. It's been so terrible, Linds. You can't imagine. Those guys call all the time on the phone, making threats. It's terrible," he repeated.

Linda stopped in her tracks and looked at him.

Ramón's eyes were shadowed with deep gray circles. He smiled, but only a little. She shifted the camera strap on her shoulder.

"I'm going to help you," Linda said.

"Yeah. How?"

"I can't tell you yet." I am absolutely going to do something today, Linda thought. Now she knew that she *was* like her mother—brave and strong, forceful and determined. She smiled. If Andrei was still around today, he was going to be sorry.

Linda turned her attention to the sidewalk itself. Through the viewfinder, everything looked so interesting. Thousands of pieces of trodden gum made a gray mosaic on the concrete. In the gutter, a group of pigeons strutted to silent music, silent rhythms. Pigeon rap. A delivery truck was unloading wooden crates of ruffle-edged lettuce, stacking them on the sidewalk. She felt the dance of daily life all around her, so she leaped into the air and tried to spin in a circle. What beautiful lettuce!

"Ooops." She bumped into Ramón. He rolled his eyes.

"See ya," she said to Ramón when they reached her corner. She waited until he was halfway down the block and then took off running for Shore Road Park, after stowing her book bag behind the garbage cans of her building on her way by. This was it.

•

The place appeared deserted as she slid down the embankment. The breeze off the bay was fresh. Tiny sprinkles of water touched her cheeks. Cautiously she approached the hideout.

"Andrei!" she yelled. "Are you in there?"

To her dismay, he poked his head out, smiled, then crawled out. He stood up and stretched, as though he'd been sleeping. Hot rage surged through Linda. "Why are you still here? I told you before, I want you out of here!" she yelled.

"No problem. Don't worry. No shouting. Okay?"

"You liar." She raised the camera and snapped his picture.

"No," he said, blocking his face with his hand. "No photo."

"Okay, no more photos. But you're leaving. Now! Get out. I mean it!"

Linda seized the blue tarp and pulled it off the roof. She wrenched loose a board and threw it into the water. The current along the bank caught it, and slowly the board moved down the bay toward the bridge. She tossed in a large piece of cardboard from a sidewall. That drifted away, too. Too bad she couldn't throw Andrei in as well.

"Stop!" shouted Andrei.

"I told the police exactly where you are and what you're doing at my school. So you'd better get out of here before they arrive. Andrei, listen! The police are coming for you. Got that?"

Linda turned and scrambled for the embankment. What a liar she was!

•

She got home thirty minutes later, picking up her book bag on the way. To her surprise, her mother said nothing. Linda grabbed a handful of Fig Newtons for a snack and ate them while she waited for her mother to hose down the entryway. Then, carefully focusing the camera, she snapped a whole series with her mother—the hose, the spray of water, her mother's furrowed, intent expression, as though the water were her weapon and not something to play with, to have fun with.

Inside, she photographed Tina playing Barbies, then Tina peeking at herself in the bathroom mirror by climbing into the sink. "Hey, Tina," Linda said, surprised. "You climb up there a lot?"

"Yeah," Tina said shyly, "but don't tell Nanë."

"I won't," Linda promised. "Your secret is safe with me." Until the Open House exhibition, that is, thought Linda. When the picture of Tina in the sink would be hanging on the wall! Tina, her mom, Andrei. What a lineup!

All through supper, Linda kept smiling to herself, remembering how she had told Andrei to get out, and thrown the board in the river. Wait till she told Ramón about it. He'd be thrilled.

•

Miss Wesley gave Linda permission to photograph Ramón in the empty classroom during Thursday's lunch period. After the eleven-fifteen bell, the eighth graders clattered out and down the stairs, and the room fell blessedly silent. Ramón poked around in his backpack and pulled out his half-crushed lunch bag. Linda quietly got out the camera, made sure it had a new roll of film inside, and looked through the lens. Visible bits of dust floated on rays of light in the air: chalk dust, kid dust, settling slowly now that the room was quiet.

Linda had Ramón sit at his desk. She wanted him to look tired, one arm draped forward across the desk, head sideways a little, tilted down. She focused on his face and then watched through the viewfinder, waiting for the right shot.

"Hey, listen. I saw Andrei yesterday. By the bay. And I told him I'd called the police and they were coming down there. Then I tore the hideout apart so he can't use it anymore."

He smiled. Linda clicked the shutter.

"That's cool," Ramón said. "So are you coming with us to the cinema tomorrow? My mother arranged for a taxi to take us. A friend of hers. So you don't have to walk or anything."

"Great. Okay."

"My mother wants to have you over for dinner sometime, too."

"Sure. Now, Ramón, look bored."

"No problem there."

The camera clicked.

"Did you get me yawning?" he asked.

"I think so."

"My mama will love these pictures. Anyway, let me tell you what we do at work so you'll be prepared. My grandmother, me, my sister, and my mother, we all go down to the cinema. First Nadia puts all the empty cans and bottles in some huge trash bags. And I wear this backpack vacuum cleaner thing. My grandmother cleans the really bad messes like sticky soda and melted candy globs. And my mother mops the floors.

"You can tell which movies are boring. No one goes to them and there's hardly any food on the floor. The cartoons are gross 'cause so many kids go to them. We get done about four and then go home and try to sleep and then I come here."

Linda took more shots. "Just a couple more, okay?"

"Yeah. Whatever."

Ramón looked different through the camera; his cheeks seemed to swallow the corners of his mouth. The hollows around his eyes seemed too dark.

"You look tired," Linda said.

"Nah. I'm okay. Listen, about my worksheets and stuff? I have to do my own work or Miss Wesley will kill us, right? So my mom has a meeting with her next week. Miss Wesley is going to get a tutor for me, a high school kid. A boy."

"Oh, okay. You think that will work out?"

"Yeah. It has to."

Through the viewfinder, Ramón still looked worried. Linda tried to think of something that would cheer him up. "Do you remember coming here to America?" she asked.

"Of course. It was only two years ago. How could I forget leaving Havana? It was my whole world. Leaving everybody. I had twenty cousins. My aunt? She was like my second mother. Remember I told you about my dad? He had a heart attack three years ago. He died right in our apartment in Havana. Boom. Like that. In the bedroom. My mother had the door closed so I couldn't see, and nobody told me for a while. Cuba has a lot of doctors, but maybe he didn't go to one. That's when my mother decided we should leave. I don't know."

Linda sat very still, the camera in her lap.

"There's no money in Cuba. If you have one dollar, you are so rich. Everyone wants to escape. Sometimes the crazy ones, they swim. Some people without a boat use inner tubes and boards. But there are sharks, and it's ninety miles to Florida. My cousin—he was nineteen—he was building a wood boat, a very small one, in the courtyard across from us. And my aunt, she's yelling every day, 'No! You can't go. You will die for sure.'

"One day, me and my cousins go down to the seawall and say goodbye to a friend of my cousin's. He was also nineteen and he made a flat boat, like a raft. We sit and watch as he leaves, as he heads out to sea. And then from nowhere at all, a big wave comes. And we see his raft go up and up, and flip upside down. Some fishing men rescue him. And my cousin goes home and destroys his boat in the courtyard."

"I'm worried about your family. I think someone should go to the police about those two guys."

"Don't tell me that. Leave this to us. To my family. It's our future that's in danger. Not yours," Ramón said angrily.

He got up abruptly and left the room as the first students wandered in after lunch. Linda sat at her desk, pulling off little pieces of her turkey sandwich and eating them, all the while staring at the floor and feeling terrible.

•

"Four by sixes, please," Linda said as she gave her film to the salesperson at the one-hour photo booth. Then she bought a Coke and a magazine and sat down to wait next to the pharmacy pickup counter.

The photos were great. There was Ramón, posing as Mr. Universe before school started. There was her mother hosing down the entryway, Tina sitting in the bathroom sink. Tina loved posing—in the dress full of pins, with her Barbies, wearing a soap-bubble beard in the kitchen. Linda had photographed her mother sewing, with her sewing basket and pincushion. She'd photographed her own nose, bulbous and close-up as though she were looking at herself in a spoon. It was a really funny picture, and Linda decided to include it in her display. Finally, there was the profile of Andrei.

At home, she straightened her blankets on her bed and then laid out the photographs. She hid the picture of Andrei in her top dresser drawer.

"Okay, Ma. Okay, Tina. The gallery is officially open."

Her mother and Tina entered the room and peered carefully at the array of photos.

"There's me, Nanë. Look. My three Barbies! There's me in the sink."

"Tina! What are you doing in that sink? I have two crazy daughters now?" their mother asked. "And look at me, with the hose. Oh, there's the sewing machine. Isn't it funny how the light shines in that one. I look all mysterious. Like an actress. Maybe you have some talent, Linda, huh? And what's this, a bag lady? Ramón's a muscleman now? Where is this? By the bay? Are you still going down there?"

"Ma. I took these before."

"All right, all right. Well, these pictures are very

good, Linda. Not what I would expect, but that's art, right?"

Linda smiled. "Yup."

19

FRIDAY NIGHT, Linda set her watch timer for 11:30 p.m. The series of tiny beeps had just started when she woke up and pushed back the lightweight summer blanket. She pulled her pajamas off. Underneath she was wearing her clothes. She leaned under her bed, groping for her sneakers, then pulled them on. She grabbed her camera and shoved two extra rolls of film into her pocket.

She opened the bedroom door. In the living room the TV was still on low. Her father was snoring in his recliner chair, where he sometimes slept all night, his head tipped back and his mouth open. She tiptoed past and very quietly opened the door. Carrying her sneakers in her hand, she stepped outside and shut the door.

She sat down by the front door and pulled on her sneakers. Now she simply had to wait for Ramón's family to meet her.

In the distance, she could see the lights of the cars whizzing by on Third Avenue, as they did day and night, but her side street was quiet.

Linda glanced at her watch. She had gotten outside quickly. It was only eleven-forty.

Linda was leaning against a tree trunk, waiting to be picked up by Mrs. Nieves's friend, who would be driving them all to the cinema in his taxi. Soon Linda saw a cab turn the corner. As it got closer, she could see Mrs. Nieves in front and the rest of the family, minus Miguel, of course, in back. She wondered how she was going to squeeze in.

The back door opened and Nadia slid over as much as possible. "Here. Sit beside me."

"Hi, everybody," Linda said as she got in.

But Ramón's mother and grandmother were in the midst of a heated argument. Periodically, the taxi driver interjected a loud comment. Linda looked at Nadia questioningly.

"Should I have stayed home?" she asked.

"This is not about you, believe me. My mother found out that Miguel is not working at any bar, that he was lying about that. And he is meeting someone tonight, probably the guy involved with the missing thousand dollars. She is really worried. And my grandmother wants her to send Miguel to live with my uncle in Miami."

Linda nodded and said nothing.

They drove the few blocks to the theater and got out. Mrs. Nieves groped in her purse for the keys and unlocked the cinema doors. Scattered all over the maroon carpet were bits of crushed popcorn, crumpled tickets, empty cups, and candy boxes.

"Wow," said Linda. "What a mess!"

"This is nothing!" Ramón opened the janitor's closet and pulled out the cleaning supplies. "Okay. There are four cinemas. We better get going. Here. Take a picture of me wearing this vacuum thing on my back. I look like something out of *Ghostbusters*."

Linda snapped Ramón a few times, and then his mother with her mop and bucket.

"How long does the whole thing take?" asked Linda. It was a little after midnight.

"Oh, usually about four hours."

Ramón switched on the vacuum cleaner. He began sucking up the popcorn, while Linda trailed after him, taking photos. A close-up of popcorn behind the display glass. A pile of ripped tickets. Nadia lugging trash bags out the back door to the Dumpster.

Then Linda photographed Ramón's grandmother, who was cleaning the ladies' room. She got what she hoped would be an interesting shot of the grandmother reflected in the long mirror above the sinks.

.

Linda wandered around for nearly two hours, until all the film was used up. For a while she followed Ramón on his way up and down the cinema aisles. Finally she flung herself into an aisle seat in theater three and leaned back with her eyes closed. She felt very sleepy. It must be so hard to do this night after night. And then go to school! How did Ramón do it?

He had just started vacuuming cinema four when they heard his mother yelling. "Why did you come here? Why? Now you're in trouble and you think your mother can help you? You should have listened to me before."

Linda and Ramón ran into the lobby. Andrei and

Miguel were standing there, breathless from running. Andrei started coughing.

"What happened?" Ramón asked.

"Those guys. They're coming for the money," Miguel said.

"Well, give it to them!" Ramón said.

"We're trying to get it back, but we don't have it yet. We lost it gambling. But we'll get it. It's just they won't wait. Listen, Ramón, they'll be here any second. We have to hide."

"Hide under the seats in cinema three. I'll lock the door."

Miguel and Andrei raced into the theater and ran down the aisle, scrambling under some seats in the middle section. Ramón flicked off the light and locked the doors.

"This is the end," his mother grumbled. "He comes in here, we're doing his work for him, and he's lost a thousand dollars. Well, after this, he's on his own. That's all." She seemed about to cry.

"Mama," Nadia said, "we have to stay calm. Like it's a normal night cleaning. In case those guys come."

"I'll be in cinema four," Ramón said. "Come on. Let's all get out of the lobby so, if they come, the place will look empty."

"The lights!" his mother exclaimed. "Where's that little light switch key? If I turn the lobby lights off, they won't know we're here."

But it was too late. There they were, banging on the door, kicking it. "Open up!"

"Oh no. They're going to break the glass," Nadia murmured. "Mama, open the door."

Her mother opened the door a crack. Linda hid her camera under her jacket, afraid they would be angry if they saw it.

Mrs. Nieves shouted, "What do you guys want? Are you going to help us clean? That would be nice."

They simply pushed past her and rushed into the lobby. Linda saw that the white guy had a small silver gun. She gasped, and they looked at her suspiciously.

"Who's this?" the Hispanic guy asked Ramón.

"My friend from school," Ramón answered. "You've seen her before."

"Where's your brother?" they asked, evidently not interested in Linda.

"I don't know."

"We saw him come in here. So don't lie. We were right behind him and that loser friend of his."

And then they all heard a door slam. Instantly the two men ran to the fire exit, the same door Nadia had used to take out the garbage, and peered out into the alley. The white guy fired two shots.

"Too late. One of them's gone. Only one of them, though. I think the Cuban must still be here. Where is he?"

Ramón shook his head, obviously trying not to cry. The white guy had come back inside and was trying all the doors. Cinema four was unlocked. Cinema three was locked. Cinemas two and one were unlocked.

"He's in three," the Hispanic guy said. "Bring the key."

Mrs. Nieves unlocked a door. Instantly, the two men were running through the rows of upturned seats. In a minute, they'd find Miguel, huddled on the floor. Linda looked desperately at Ramón.

Then, suddenly, Miguel jumped up, leaping straight over the row in front of him, bolting for the fire exit at the front of the theater.

The white guy shot once, but Miguel kept running. Down the aisle now, he was only twenty feet from the exit. The white guy shot again. And Miguel fell forward, to the floor. Ramón and Nadia screamed. Then Nadia ran for the phone in the manager's office to call for help. Ramón and Linda ran down the aisle to Miguel. The two men shoved open the fire door and disappeared into the alley.

And now, thought Linda, the police would come. She'd be caught here, where there were criminals, shootings, stolen money. Her family was illegal. She couldn't get involved with police. What on earth should she do? Should she hide? She looked around frantically. No. She straightened up. The answer was suddenly clear to her. The hidden photo of Andrei. Her own family. They must be made to understand.

"Ramón, I'm leaving. I'm going home," she said.

Ramón looked up at her. But before he could speak, Linda slipped through the exit and took off, running.

20

SHE ARRIVED HOME, gasping, and with trembling fingers locked the door behind her, fearing irrationally that somehow one of the men might have followed her. "Mom! Dad! I need help!" she called out. "Ma!"

Had Nadia gotten through to the police? Linda couldn't be sure. She dialed 911. Then: "Hello? This— Um, this is an emergency. Someone was shot in the Bay Ridge multiplex. Near Seventy-ninth Street."

"Your name, miss?" the dispatcher asked.

Linda didn't answer. Instead she said, "You have to send someone right away. The police, too. I heard screaming and shooting."

"All right, we've got someone on the way. Now. Your name."

Her parents came into the hall, staring at her.

"I—I can't tell you."

"You have to tell us so we can file a report."

"But I'm not allowed to tell you. I mean, I'll get in a lot of trouble . . . My mother doesn't want . . ." She had no idea what to say.

Her mother said, "Give me the phone, Linda."

"I have to go now," she said. "My mom will talk to you."

Her mother took the receiver and spoke. "Her name is Linda Berati. Age thirteen. Telephone number is—"

"We have your number already. We'll send a detective by in the morning."

Her mother hung up.

"It seems, Linda, you have something to tell us," she said.

"Yeah." She leaned against her mother and hugged her.

"Come in the living room and sit down," her mother said. Her dad turned off the TV and sat in the recliner.

"This week at school . . . Well, I saw this guy selling drugs in front of Mullaney."

"Yes, go ahead."

"And I knew who it was. I didn't want anybody to get in trouble. Especially Ramón, so—"

"Wait a minute, Linda," her father said. "I'm not following this. Start over."

So Linda told her parents as much detail about Andrei and Miguel as she could remember. "They— Well, Andrei has been using my hideout near the bay."

Her father laughed.

"It's not funny, Dad. It was a great hideout, but I had to tear it apart."

Linda looked at her watch and was surprised to see that the time was only 2:45. She felt as if she'd been gone all night.

"I was going with the Nieves family to their job tonight, remember? And we were at the cinema, when suddenly Miguel and Andrei burst in, trying to hide. Then these two guys came, drug dealers or something. They'd been looking for Miguel since last week. And they said Miguel owed them a lot of money. Andrei ran out the back. And there was a gunshot. They shot Miguel. I was so, so scared. So I came home and called the police. Andrei is this terrible guy. He's a complete liar. Anyway, he escaped. But I have a photo of him. Here. I'll get it. We can give it to the detective, I guess."

Linda hurried to her bedroom and got the photograph from her top dresser drawer. She handed it to her father, who studied the picture carefully. Andrei was turned partly away from the camera, but his dark hair, thin, wiry form, and sharply hooked nose made him clearly identifiable.

"Unbelievable," her father said. "How long has this been going on, with this guy down there?"

"A couple of weeks. Since just before school started," Linda said, feeling her face flush.

"Why didn't you tell us, Linda?" her mother asked. "Dear God! You could have been killed."

"I don't know. Ramón said his family could handle it. I thought I could handle it." Linda sank down lower on the velvet sofa cushions and slipped the camera off over her head.

"But why didn't you tell us about the guy in your hideout?" her father asked.

"Because . . . well, at first I felt sorry for him. I thought he was like us—you know, just illegal. I didn't know he was selling drugs or anything. Then I couldn't call the cops. Ma said we could never tell the police anything," Linda said. "I was so afraid the police might come here. I mean, that would be terrible, right? So I was stuck keeping everything a secret."

"All right!" her mother said. She stood up. "That's it. We are not going to live like this anymore. So afraid of the police that we put ourselves in real danger. We came here to be free, not to be afraid."

"Of course we can call the police," Linda's father said firmly. "They don't ask for visas, Tefta. Trust me for once."

Linda looked at her mother. "But, Nanë? I need you to trust me. At least a little. Dad? Okay?"

"You wait here. We'll be back," her mother said, and her parents left the room.

•

They were gone for a surprisingly long time. Linda could hear her parents' low voices in their bedroom as they talked and talked. The empty living room felt comfortable and peaceful. Linda sank back on the sofa, closing her tired eyes. It was long after three now. She wasn't sure she had ever stayed up this late before.

At last her mother and father came in, and her mother sat next to Linda. It was a moment before Linda realized that she was crying. Linda had never seen her really cry before. She cried not soft sobs but harsh, wrenching gasps torn from her chest. She covered her face with her hands and rocked back and forth with grief.

"Ma? What?" said Linda. "What is it?"

Linda wrapped her arms around her mother's neck and held on tight. "Don't cry, Ma," she whispered. "And please don't yell at me anymore. I'm safe now. I'm safe here." Then she remembered what Miss Wesley had said. "I won't suffer the way you had to, Ma. I'll be okay. Life won't be so terrible for me."

"I just don't want you in any danger. After all we went

through. I yell at you to keep you safe," her mother said. "Now you tell us this awful thing. You could have been killed."

"But yelling at me doesn't make me safe. And, Ma, I have to try things for myself. I have to learn," Linda said.

"You have to be more open with us," her father said. "We have to trust you one hundred percent."

Linda nodded.

"But we can't live in a situation where our daughters can't be open with us. America doesn't work like that," her father said.

"No. I know," her mother said. "Your father and I have been talking. As you know, your teacher has called here, and I can tell from her voice that she will call again."

Linda smiled to herself, imagining Buns of Steel penetrating the rocky walls of her mother's mind.

"She doesn't think that the eighth-grade program is right for you at Mullaney. I never heard of such a thing. A school not right for someone. She said Donna is now friends with many boys. Is that right? A flirt?"

Linda shrugged. "Yeah. I guess."

"And your teacher said you spend your time drawing silly pictures like Ramón does."

"Yeah. Sometimes." Linda blushed at this description of herself. Surely Miss Wesley had said something positive about her!

"What a waste of time. You girls don't appreciate—"

"Anyway," her father cut in, "I will call the director of that academy and arrange for you to visit this Clemens to see if you like it. But you must promise us that you'll study very hard there. No more running around, chasing drug dealers, and so on. Understand?"

Linda nodded.

Was it possible that Buns of Steel had truly come through for her? That was so great. Adults were amazing and weird and complicated all at once. A perfect example, Buns was wonderful and awful at the same time. And so was her mother.

And she, Linda, was going to become one of those crazy, mixed-up grownups herself! The zits, the curves, the Weird Me feelings, the stuff kids focused on and shrieked about were in fact nothing, simply stepping-stones on the path to this ultimate destiny of power and stubbornness—adulthood.

How awful! Linda sank lower in her chair and tried to smile. "Thanks, guys. Will we ever be legal, though?"

"I don't know," said her father gravely. "We can't do anything about that. But as long as we're in this country, I want you to study. No matter where we end up, that's the most important thing."

Linda knew that. Now she did smile.

21

NADIA OPENED THE DOOR to their spotlessly clean apartment. She was wearing a black skirt and frilly white blouse and her hair was piled up in curly wisps on her head.

Crepe paper was strung from the corners of the room and tied in a big bow in the middle. "Welcome!" she called out.

"What is this?" asked Linda. "You look so nice."

"Just a little party for you. My mother wants to say thank you for coming with us to help Ramón in school. He got a B-plus on his report—not an A-plus, like you, but pretty good. Miss Wesley arranged for a tutor for him after school, Tuesdays and Thursdays. Isn't that great? So. Anyway. Come in, come in. Look at the new sofa. Well, only from Goodwill. Our uncle bought it for us when he came from Miami."

Ramón's mother came forward and took Linda's hand. She led her to the new sofa, which was really the only place in the nearly empty living room to sit down. The grandmother sat in one of the three kitchen chairs. Nadia went into the kitchen and came out with a tray and three glasses of soda—one for herself, one for Ramón, and one for Linda. Linda could see a plateful of little sandwiches and a cake in the kitchen. She knew that the family didn't have a job right now. How had they bought so much food? Perhaps their uncle had left some money as well.

"*Hola,*" she said to Ramón's grandmother, smiling. "*Gracias.*"

"Very good, very good," said Ramón's grandmother, nodding and patting her knee.

"*Muchas gracias,*" said Linda, encouraged at her success.

Ramón's grandmother threw back her head and laughed. His mother smiled and said, "We were fired from the cinema after what happened. Miguel has gone to stay with my brother in Miami. He runs a small construction business down there. He'll put Miguel to work. No one argues long with my brother."

"I'm sorry about your cinema job," Linda said.

"Oh, phhht," said Ramón's mother. "We'll find something else. It was no good for Ramón, being up in the middle of the night, being sleepy every day in school."

"I don't know how Ramón managed to go to school like that. I was so tired after that one night at the cinema. Hey, Ramón, how did things go with your tutor, anyway?" Linda asked.

Ramón made a face. "Okay, I guess. But he makes me do the work myself, not like you. I'm going to meet with him twice a week. Did you notice? I turned in my grammar sheet on time."

Linda laughed. "Yeah, I noticed. So, I mean, about Miguel . . . did the police arrest him?"

Nadia waved her hand in disgust. "We're all so angry with him. No. The police actually came to the emergency ward and questioned him. His wound was nothing much, it turned out. The bullet just grazed his shoulder. But what could they arrest him for? And those two guys were gone long before the police arrived at the cinema. So." She shrugged. "My mother told Miguel that *she* knew he was guilty—of selling drugs, stealing that money, and God knows what else—even if the police did nothing to him. My uncle flew up here Sunday and there was another big fight—"

"Hopefully the last big fight," Ramón broke in.

"And my uncle is going to make Miguel work in his construction business in Florida. Paving. Hot tar."

"Yeah! Thank God for that," said Ramón. "Plus I get the whole sofa bed to myself."

"Hey. He's your brother. You're going to miss him, right?" Nadia said.

"Right! And I sure won't miss those two guys."

"Me neither," said Nadia. "They won't come back now that Miguel's gone. What is that expression? You can't get blood from a stone."

After they had eaten the sandwiches, Ramón's mother brought in the cake and set it in front of Linda.

"To another new beginning, Linda. Ever since we came here, that's all we do. Make new beginnings. But what's so bad about that, huh?" Ramón's mother smiled and cut Linda a big slice.

"How about we go to Geppetto's afterward. Do you like coffee, Linda?" Nadia asked.

Linda glanced at Ramón and laughed. "Only cappuccino."

•

Linda entered the small admissions office at Clemens Academy, her camera over her shoulder. She was wearing her usual clunky jewelry, work boots, and overalls despite her mother's repeated demands that she wear a dress. Relax, she told herself. How can it possibly be worse than Mullaney Junior High?

A tall girl with her hair wrapped in a colorful scarf got up to greet her.

"Hi. I'm Kira. You're Linda, right? I'm going to give

you your tour. Feel free to ask me anything 'cause I know it can all seem confusing at first. About the core courses, electives, and everything. Ready?"

Feel free, Linda thought, smiling. Great words. A great feeling. She felt as though she had finally stepped out of Donna's suffocating, pink-striped bedroom into a wide-open prairie. Maybe she was done with her life of hanging out in a hideout, feeling trapped and isolated. And as for the uncertainty of her future, she couldn't live her life afraid of it. She would step boldly forward no matter what.

"What?" asked Kira, seeing Linda's smile.

"Oh, nothing. I'm just excited to be here."

"Yeah? Great." Kira laughed. "Let's go, then. Let the tour begin."